Really Angelic

'Pride and Prejudice' with a paranormal twist

By

ENID WILSON

To

Mei and Michael

Enid Wilson loves sexy romance. Her writing career began with a daily newspaper, writing educational advice for students. She then branches out into writing marketing materials and advertising copies. Enid's novels *In Quest of Theta Magic* and *Bargain with the Devil*, received several top reviews. Enid loves to hear from her readers. You can contact her at enid.wilson28@yahoo.com.au or www.steamydarcy.com

Illustration and cover design by Z. Diaz

First published 2009

CHAPTER ONE

1801

Elizabeth Bennet was a happy, cheery girl. To the delight of her father, she loved to read and showed sign of intelligence. But to the dismay of her mother, she loved the countryside too much. She seemed always to be running about, playing with animals and climbing trees.

Her mischief often landed her sisters and friends in difficult situations. One of those circumstances occurred when she was ten years old.

It was a bright summer day. Elizabeth was playing, together with her neighbour Luke Lucas and her younger sister Kitty, near the main road to London.

"Let us play throw," Elizabeth challenged Luke. He was the elder by two years but had only grown taller than she was in the past few months. His new vertical advantage was a fact she disliked a great deal.

She picked up a small piece of rock from the ground and pointed to the tall oak tree. "Whoever's stone reaches a branch taller will be the victor."

Kitty clapped her hands with delight and agreed to the game. Luke shook his head. "I do not want to play with girls," he said and continued to kick the tree absently.

Elizabeth stepped closer. "What do you have against girls?"

"You make mischief and put the blame on me if we are found out."

"I do no such thing!" Her hands were fisted on her hips. "You are only afraid that I can throw higher than you."

"It is a stupid game anyway," he replied and started towards his house.

Kitty looked at her sister with a frown and decided to follow Luke.

"Coward!" Elizabeth shouted after them. "Traitor!" She stalked off in the opposite direction. Bending down to pick up stones, she threw them aimlessly to vent her frustration for nearly quarter of an hour. She was nearer to the main road than she had realised and did not, in her temper, notice that a grand carriage was passing by.

Her last throw struck one of the horses.

The steed startled, reared up. The driver was unable to control the other horses, with the result that the carriage tipped to one side and crashed noisily to the roadway.

Screams and yells emanated from within it. Then within seconds, silence returned again.

With her hands over her mouth, Elizabeth stood frozen on the spot. Her first instinct was to run home and hide. She had killed an entire carriage of innocent people!

But then moans became audible. Elizabeth ran nearer to the source and saw that the sounds came from a young man sprawled in the roadway with one of his legs trapped beneath the top edge of the carriage. He was tall, she noted, with dark curly hair. His feature was very handsome and he was immaculately dressed.

"Are you well, sir?" Elizabeth asked in a trembling voice.

"How are my men?" he asked. She left him and ran to check on other men – four of them – strewn upon the roadway.

"They are unconscious but breathing," she reported back to him.

"Help me get free then. I need to see to them." He struggled to get his leg out but the carriage would not move. He gave a shout of pain and frustration, and then looked askance at Elizabeth's form. "You are too small. Perhaps you had best run and ask for help."

She shook her head. "I must help you. I accidentally startled your horse. I am truly sorry," she admitted, with tears in her eyes.

She then put her small hands beneath the roof of the carriage. With a sudden surge of energy and a loud scream, she lifted the tip of the carriage up from the ground by several inches.

Both of them were flabbergasted by her strength. When the young man did not immediately move, she yelled, "Pull your leg out. I cannot hold it any longer."

He moved back immediately and pulled his leg free, just before she gave out another scream and let the carriage drop back to the ground. Stunned, she sank down beside the young man, panting heavily.

"However did you summon such strength?" he asked, gazing at her in astonishment.

She shook her head. "I do not know."

Before she could stand up and help him, she heard another carriage approaching. As soon as she glimpsed it, she knew that it bore Sir William Lucas, and she felt a thrill of panic. Surely he would tell her parents.

She said quickly to the young man, "I am truly sorry about this incident. I hope your servants will recover soon." Then she scrambled away from him.

"Wait!" he called after her. "What is your name?"

She only shook her head and ran to hide in the bushes. Once concealed, she waited until Sir William and his servant had taken care of the young man and the men who had accompanied him before she turned, at last, and returned home. Her mother scolded her for making her dress such a mess and for coming home late.

Elizabeth later learned from local gossip that the young man was called Mr. Fitzwilliam Darcy of Pemberley, and that he was from Derbyshire. By the public account, he and his servants were well enough to take another carriage and continue their journey to London four days later. She was relieved to find that Mr. Darcy had made no mention of a young girl's involvement in the accident.

At first, Elizabeth thought back upon that incident with shame and incredulity. She later tried lifting heavy objects, on several occasions, but the Herculean strength of that disastrous day never returned to her. Slowly, with the passage of time, she forgot about the whole debacle.

However, the accident immediately sprang back to her mind on the day, ten years later, when she encountered Mr. Darcy again – this time at the local Assembly. Evidently he had come to visit his friend Mr. Charles Bingley, who had recently rented Netherfield Park, which was located only three miles from her home.

***

1811

Mr. Darcy's appearance at the Meryton Assembly drew marked attention. Sir William Lucas remembered the young man whom he had rescued some ten years earlier, and he did not hesitate to declare him as his friend. But Mr. Darcy was reserved and distant in his manner. He bore with the people to whom Sir William introduced him, answering direct questions about his long-ago injury and his well-being since that time. However he did not engage in extended conversation or dance much throughout the night.

It seemed apparent that Mr. Darcy had grown into a fastidious and arrogant man. *He is no longer the caring master who worried more about his men's safety than his own. And he finds me not handsome enough to dance with. Well then, I shall not waste my time upon him.* Elizabeth decided as she walked purposely very near to him and then crossed to talk with her good friend Charlotte Lucas.

She told Charlotte about his haughty remark concerning her not being handsome enough to dance with, and the two young women had a good laugh together. Elizabeth noted that their playful manner seemed to attract his attention, but not in any positive sense. Indeed, his gaze conveyed censure and a frosty disapproval.

He must think us savages, without any refined manner. I wish he would overset a wineglass upon himself. That would certainly make him less handsome, at least for a moment!

Within moments, it seemed, Mr. Darcy had moved over to the refreshment table, where he did indeed pick up a glass of wine. At the same instant, Elizabeth's youngest sister, Lydia, dashed past him in her haste to greet a local boy. She knocked against his elbow as she passed, with the result that he tipped the wine over his fine clothes. Due to the crowded room and her preoccupation, Lydia did not even notice the mischief she had dealt the man.

With a scowl at the young girl, Mr. Darcy took out a handkerchief and tried to absorb the stain. Mr. Bingley's sister, Caroline, rushed to his side. She sympathised with the gentleman's mishap. When she raised her gloved hand and attempted, with a napkin, to help him wipe away the wine, Mr. Darcy backed away. He bowed to her abruptly, turned on his heel, and left the hall for the back room.

Elizabeth watched the entire sequence of events with uneasy wonder. *Did that happen because I wished for it?* She wondered, but she could not bring herself to believe it. *Why do strange things happen when I am around Mr. Darcy? Should I follow the man and attempt to apologise to him? If I do, surely he will think me a mad woman.*

She decided, instead, to venture out onto the balcony for some much-needed air.

Gaining the relative privacy of the balcony, Elizabeth was startled to find that the weather had changed. Earlier in the evening, when she arrived at the Assembly with her family, it had been warm and calm. Now, the wind was picking up sharply, and the clouds were travelling fast.

She rubbed her hands over her arms and decided that she had best return to the ballroom. It was altogether too cold and windy on the balcony for comfort. Her hair and dress would be a sight if she lingered there for long.

As she turned to leave the balcony, a flash of lightning pierced the sky, and a rough gust of wind shouldered through the tall trees.

Ching!

The sharp sound of an object dropping onto the balcony floor attracted her attention. She turned back, narrowing her eyes to keep them open against the strong wind.

On the stone floor by her feet was a tiny shiny item. She bent to retrieve it, then walked quickly back into the room.

Moving to a quiet corner, she examined the object. It was a quill...but a strange one. The length was about two-thirds that of a normal writing quill. The feather itself was in the most extraordinary hues of blue. The barrel was exceptionally thick. And at the tip was a piece of metal, apparently affixed to protect the sharp point.

She stroke along the feather, and a sudden answering shiver ran through her body. The unexpected sensation made her press the barrel harder than she intended, and several drops of golden liquid dripped from its tip. It looked much like ink but when she put her fingertip out to touch it, the liquid evaporated immediately.

A quill filled with golden ink that vanishes? Very strange indeed! Where did it come from? Who made it? She could not think of a single plausible answer. Stymied, she decided to tuck the quill away so that she could examine it more closely later.

***

The night ended triumphantly for the Bennet family, for the rich Mr. Bingley had shown marked interest in Jane Bennet, Elizabeth's eldest sister, and he had danced with her several times. Mrs. Fanny Bennet, however, was cross with Mr. Darcy over his slight of her Elizabeth. With their own estate entailed away and no male heir in sight, the Mistress of Longbourn had made it her avowed mission to marry off her daughters to rich men.

When, after a short, happy discussion concerning the successful Assembly, the family retired to their respective bed chambers, Elizabeth found that she was still alarmed by the events of the night. First, the belated re-appearance of Mr. Darcy after a ten-year hiatus was highly unusual. Second, his tipping over of the wine as if in direct accordance with her wishes was as unbelievable as it was undeniable. And thirdly, the discovery of the brilliant blue quill filled with vanishing ink was a puzzle that defied her not inconsiderable intellectual prowess.

She did not feel at all ready to sleep, and so she took out the quill from her reticule in order to examine it further. Sitting down at her little writing desk, she placed the tip against a fresh piece of paper and attempted to draw with it. But no golden liquid was forthcoming, and nothing appeared on the paper.

Biting her lip, she shook the quill and pressed the barrel more firmly before starting to draw with it again. Still the paper remained blank.

Before she decided to take out her usual inkwell and dip the special quill into it, she made one last effort, this time trying to write her name: *Elizabeth Bennet*.

It worked! Her name appeared neatly in gold on the paper.

How very strange! Perhaps the quill with golden ink only works when writing names. With a shake of her head, she wrote again: *Jane Bennet.* But no ink was forthcoming. Jane's name was invisible.

Strange, indeed! One after another, she made a try of her parents' names, then of Mary, Kitty, Lydia, Charlotte and others, but none produced visible results.

With a sigh of frustration, she considered abandoning her efforts to solve the mystery in favor of simply going to sleep. But her own name was still visible, golden and glistening in the light from her candle.

A sudden gust of wind outside rattled the trees, producing an eerie sound that reminded her of what she had heard on the balcony during the evening she had spent with the newcomers in the neighbourhood.

Freshly inspired, she wrote out the names of the Bingley party: Mr. Bingley, his sister Mrs. Hurst, her husband Mr. Hurst, and his other sister Miss Bingley. Still no words were visible on paper.

Thus far, Elizabeth had deliberately reframed from writing Mr. Darcy's name. At last, however, when no other prospect presented itself, she attempted his name, with a shaking hand: *Mr. Darcy.*

The two words appeared under her name, firm and sparkling.

How can that be? Why does the magic quill work only with his name and mine? What can it mean? Is it...magic? Disquieted by the thought, she told herself sternly, *more likely the quill is simply defective.* Elizabeth dropped the quill on the table with a sigh of frustration.

Abruptly, lightning flashed, brightening the room. It illumined the quill, from which a puff of blue smoke emerged.

Elizabeth backed away from the table hastily and scrambled onto the bed. Seconds later, when the smoke dissipated, she was stunned by the sight of a man standing inside her room, near the window.

She opened her mouth to scream but the man raised his hand, and not a word came out from her mouth.

"Do not scream!" the man said. "I do not intend to bring harm."

Elizabeth trembled as she took in his attire. He was wearing a long blue robe that covered his body from neck to toe. The fabric looked like silk, smooth and shiny, with a cloud depicted in white on the front. The unfamiliar man was tall, with long blond hair.

Elizabeth scrambled under the sheet and gathered the bed clothes to cover her body. She was only wearing a night gown and did not intend to expose herself to a stranger's view.

After swallowing several times to calm herself, she managed to suppress the urge to scream. Gathering her wits, she said, "I demand you to leave my bed chamber immediately, sir. It is most improper for you to…visit me here."

He raised his hand and pressed it to his forehead. "I do apologise. I forgot the restrictions of your society. I will change so that you will feel more comfortable speaking to me."

Change? Comfortable? She wanted to protest that she could never feel comfortable speaking with a stranger who appeared out of thin air...

Before she could say a word, another puff of smoke erupted, and the mysterious man…turned into a woman. The blond hair was still long and unbound, but the facial features and body were now clearly womanly.

Is he – no, she – a ghost? Elizabeth, having already experienced too many strange happenstances in a single night, swooned. The last word she heard was spoken by the ghost in a tone of undisguised exasperation: "Women!"

CHAPTER TWO

Something cold… Something wet…

Elizabeth blinked rapidly, struggling to wake up. When she opened her eyes, she was shocked to see that the ghost was still there. In fact, the blond woman was splashing drops of water onto her face!

Senses reeling, Elizabeth closed her eyes, hoping to escape back into oblivion and shut out the evil spirit, but the ghost exclaimed, "Do not swoon! I am no ghost. I am an angel. And I have no time to wait again for you to wake up. I have had a most tiring day."

An angel? Then what is she doing here in my room? Elizabeth gathered her courage and raised herself higher, sitting up in bed. "What are you doing here?" she asked.

"I have come for you," the angel said.

Elizabeth gasped, then asked in an unsteady voice, "Am I about to die? Have you come to bring me to Heaven?"

"No such thing. You have it all wrong. You are one of us."

"One of you? Whatever do you mean?"

"You are an angel, too."

At that, Elizabeth laughed out loud. "Your jest is a foolish one!" This was the first moment in which she had truly felt like herself since re-encountering Mr. Darcy. "I am Elizabeth Bennet, second daughter of Mr. Bennet from Longbourn of Hertfordshire. I assure you that, quite justifiably, I have never been called an 'angel' in my entire life. Are you sure you do not want to speak with my elder sister, Jane? I remember hearing Mr. Bingley call her an angel earlier tonight."

"I am most serious," the angel protested. "I am Michael. And you are *Lizzybell*." She shook her head and continued, "No, in female form as I am now, I suppose you must call me Mihaela."

Elizabeth continued to laugh, "*Lizzybell*? What an awful name for an angel! I am sure I have never read of an angel with such a name."

"You are a level-six angel. No one in *Himins* gives level-six angels proper attention." Mihaela grimaced. "I do admit, your name is a trifle horrible."

"*Himins*?"

"It is the correct name for what you on Earth call 'Heaven'," Mihaela said. "But let us not begin on the history of *Himins*. I am pressed for time. I need to tell you why I am here and what you need to do."

Elizabeth nodded her head, since protesting seemed to do no good. She did not in the least understand what was happening. Perhaps it was all a dream.

"I work in the Lost Angel Commission. You dropped from *Himins* through a crack in the sky. It took me some time to track you down. I need to arm you with knowledge and skill about *Himins* so that you can return to us at the next opportunity."

"Now I know that you jest," Elizabeth stated with conviction. "What sort of Heaven is that, where an angel can be lost and simply drop from the sky?"

"Well, let us say that matters are a bit more chaotic than what can be learned from reading Greek mythology," Mihaela said. "On the day you fell into the woods near Pemberley, *Zenobie* was arguing with his wife. He stomped his foot a bit too heavily and thus a crack occurred. As a result, several low-level angels descended precipitously to Earth."

Elizabeth peered in consternation at the crazy angel. It was, after all, very late and she had had a traumatic day. But did notice something important. "Pemberley? But that is Mr. Darcy's estate!"

"Yes, and that is where Mrs. Bennet found you, twenty years ago, in the woods near Pemberley."

Mother is not my mother? "Is that why strange things happened when I was in the company of Mr. Darcy?" Elizabeth asked, "Because I ... dropped onto his land?"

"No, indeed not." Mihaela shook her head and started pacing. "It is because you are his guardian angel. But I really have no time now. I must chase after another lost angel."

"Guardian angel?" Elizabeth repeated in astonishment. "Wait! You cannot leave me without further explanation!"

Mihaela turned back long enough to thrust the quill at her. "Use the angelic *petna*. Simply write down your question and chant '*instructio andswara*,' and you shall receive answers to most of your questions." She then raised her body and flew out of the window and hovered there long enough to call to Elizabeth, "I shall come back to teach you more angelic skills so that you can return to *Himins* when the time comes. In the mean time, you have to guard your ward on Earth."

Elizabeth stared after her with wide eyes. "And so I am to believe that angels do not have wings?" she said aloud to the four walls of her bedchamber. "I truly must be dreaming." And with that, exhausted, she lowered her head onto the pillow and closed her eyes.

***

Elizabeth woke to the familiar sound of Jane's voice.

"Lizzy, it is almost time for breakfast. I have never known you to sleep so late. Are you unwell?" Gently, she shook Elizabeth's shoulder.

Elizabeth blinked several times to adjust to the bright sunlight streaming into the room. "I have been dreaming too much," she said, and raised herself on the bed.

"Were they sweet dreams?"

"Perhaps," Elizabeth replied in some perplexity. "I cannot seem to remember just now."

"Well, come down soon. You do not want to be late for breakfast." And with that, Jane left Elizabeth's room.

Slowly, Elizabeth began to remember the strange happenings of the previous night. Rising, she went to examine the paper on the table. Mr. Darcy's and her name were no long visible. So! It had only been a peculiar dream, angel and all!

But when she pulled open the drawer under the mirror to put the unused paper away, she found the angelic blue quill awaiting her there.

Her heart began to race. *Am I to believe, then that it was no dream? But I do not want to be angel. I just want to be Lizzy!*

She groaned. Perhaps the quill wrote normally, after all. She scribbled with it but, as on the previous night, no ink came out. Steeling herself she then wrote, *'I am Mr. Darcy's guardian angel.'*

The words gleamed golden on the pale paper.

Lizzy bit her lip. Deciding that ignorance was no shield, she softly chanted, "*Instructio andswara,*" and then wrote, *'What are the duties of a guardian angel?'*

A sudden succession of words materialised on the sheet.

Lizzy gasped and backed away from the table, dropping the *petna* on the floor. Then, cautiously, she took a few deep breathes and moved forward to read the words on the paper.

'Praise, reveal, guide, provide, protect, deliver and encourage.

Fulfill your duties and win elevation.

Neglect your obligations and risk reparation.'

She gasped. *Are those words for me? Surely no one will say I neglect my responsibilities. I did not even know I was an angel.* Picking up the quill, she was about to touch it to the white surface again when she heard her mother's loud voice demanding her presence downstairs.

With a heavy sigh, Lizzy placed the angelic instrument and the paper into her treasure box, locked them there, and hurried to dress.

Soon thereafter, when she sat down at the table amid the loud chatter of her family, the reality struck her with unexpected force. She would have to leave them all, one day. *But how can I live without Father, Jane, Aunt and Uncle Gardiner? Even Mother and my younger sisters' silly ways will be missed. Can I refuse to return to Heaven? Or, rather, to Himins. Will Mr. Darcy suffer if I am not there to protect him? Has he suffered in the past twenty years? Who will deal me reparation?*

"You are very quiet today, Lizzy." Mr. Bennet said.

"Well, small wonder! I should be devastated too," Mrs. Bennet exclaimed, "if I were told I was not handsome enough to dance with, that hateful Mr. Darcy! How dare he slight our Lizzy?"

"You are not so missish as to take offence, are you, daughter?" her father asked.

Elizabeth was about to agree with her mother that Mr. Darcy was the most arrogant man she had ever met…when she suddenly remembered that one of her roles as guardian angel was to praise. "Perhaps he received bad tidings from his family. His words might sound harsh, but should we not be more Christian and grant him the benefit of the doubt?"

"How droll, Lizzy!" Lydia laughed out loud, "You sound like Mary now."

"No, she speaks like Jane," Kitty observed, and added, "It does not suit you!"

Elizabeth turned bright red at her younger sisters' remarks. Although her father and Jane chastised them, Elizabeth was embarrassed by the reception that her first angelic attempt had received.

***

The ladies of Longbourn soon waited on those of Netherfield, and the visit was returned in due form. After Elizabeth encountered Mr. Darcy a few times during these short visits, she decided to avoid his acquaintance until she could better master the subject of angels. But that did not prevent her from observing him from afar.

His quiet, reserved and unsociable demeanour made people believe he had grown to be conceited and arrogant. His public slight of Elizabeth, one of the area's much-loved local beauties, added further to his unpopularity. Residents marveled at the special friendship between the most amiable Mr. Bingley and the disdainful Mr. Darcy. While the presence of such an illustrious character made the small community buzz with gossip and debates, the Derbyshire man did not win any approval or make any new friends.

Elizabeth monitored the situation with concern and frustration. On the one hand, she acknowledged a huge task ahead. Mr. Darcy would surely lead a sad life if he only befriended people like Miss Bingley, a young woman who soothed his ego without reason and faked her affection, all because of his wealth.

On the other hand, Elizabeth could not bring herself to like the man. He often hurt people's feelings by not engaging in conversations or by making sharp, condescending remarks. He might well be speaking the truth, but he could benefit from learning some finesse and tact as well.

The situation troubled her deeply, for how was she to bear a task that concerned a man she could neither like nor admire?

Elizabeth used whatever time she had alone to study the subject of angels. She was alarmed by many of the differences she found between her experience of angels and the ones that she read of in religious stories. On the subject of her ward, however, the magic quill said simply that she would have to discover her obligations as she went along.

Now that she was more knowledgeable about her station, she decided to better acquaint herself with him. She discovered at Sir William's gathering that Mr. Darcy seemed to enjoy listening to her conversations with other people. But why? Did he want to identify faults about her? Or was his goal to intimidate her?

"What could he possibly be about," Charlotte asked, "by listening to your conversation with Colonel Forster so attentively?"

"I have no idea," Elizabeth said truthfully. However, rather than voicing her bleak suspicion, she took a more objective approach. "Perhaps he wanted to introduce the topic of the war with the Colonel but was reluctant to interrupt my teasing the Colonel to give us a ball."

Then she nearly forgot what she was talking about, upon seeing Mr. Darcy approaching her again, though he seemed not to have any intention of speaking. Instead, he stood next to Charlotte and her, close enough to overhear them easily.

Elizabeth decided to start teaching him the skill of being a gentleman and engaging in conversation. She turned to him with her warmest smile. "Sir, you heard me just now speaking of the benefits of our Majesty's militia hosting a ball for the locals," she said and added archly, "Do you not agree that Hertfordshire ladies are as well-informed as those in town?"

"Nearly all ladies are enlightened on this subject – by which I mean the ball, not the war." He gave her a quick glance as he replied, but he neither turned to face her nor returned her smile.

"You have quite a satirical view of us!" she said, and thought privately, *I cannot understand the man. I have already graced him with my brightest smile. What more can I do to make him happy?*

"You must show him that we are also well-educated on music." Charlotte said. "I am going to open the piano and you know what follows." She then walked away from the pair.

"She is such a strange creature, always wanting me to exhibit in front of people." Elizabeth was about to put down her drink by the refreshment table and prepare to play when she felt Mr. Darcy's elbow bump her arm suddenly, causing wine to spill down the front of her dress. Feeling the cold liquid slide down her bosom, quite ruining the bodice of her gown, she gasped.

Mr. Darcy turned to face her. His eyes focused on her cleavage for a minute, eyeing the dampened muslin. His face turned bright red and he murmured, "I am extremely sorry. Pray forgive me. I should not have thought... " Then he bowed and left abruptly.

She could not believe such an accident could happen twice. She put down her glass and took another from the table and, rebelliously, downed the contents in a serious of bold swallows. *I do not want to be an angel!*

***

Elizabeth blotted the damage to her gown as best she could, which was not very well at all. When she displayed the evidence of the mishap to her mother and begged to go home early, her mother stubbornly disagreed. She would not hear of leaving the gathering now, just when things were going so well between Mr. Bingley and Jane.

Fortunately, Charlotte came to her rescue. She took Elizabeth to her room and asked the maid to dry her clothes. They chatted while they waited. But that did not save Elizabeth from experiencing a huge headache.

Immediately after the Bennets reached home, Elizabeth excused herself and went to her bedchamber, wishing nothing more than to nurse her headache with a good sleep, but she was in for a surprise: Mihaela, the 'Missing Angel Commissioner,' decided to visit her again.

"What do you want now?" Elizabeth demanded with some annoyance. She reclined on the bed, not bothering to raise and greet the angel properly.

"I want to make sure you have been learning your way with the *petna*," Mihaela said.

"Well, I have learned a fair bit about *Himins* and my jobs from it. But I know not how I am to protect Mr. Darcy, nor have I developed any angelic skills."

"Then I will teach you some, now."

"But I am tired and I have a headache," Elizabeth said with a sigh. "Can we not leave it for another day?"

"There is no skirting of your duties, young thing." Mihaela said, turning into Michael and speaking in a deep, serious voice.

Elizabeth recoiled, still uneasy over having a man in her room, even if he was an angel.

"Very well then, sir." She put on a robe and said, "But can you change back to Mihaela?"

"You are an impertinent low-level angel." He scowled but complied with her request, returning to his female form. "Nevertheless, I shall now teach you how to fly."

Elizabeth asked in awe, "So I have wings?"

"Yes, they are embedded inside your bone but you can only use them when you come to your ward's rescue or request," Mihaela said. "Simply roll your shoulders, left, right and left, then chant '*Crosswind and Whirlwind, I trust Ventara, the God of Wind.*' Wings will then spring out from the back of your neck."

Elizabeth wanted to laugh at the silly chant but she could see that the Commissioner was losing patience. She did as she was told and to her complete astonishment, she felt a strong tickling at the base of her neck and suddenly her skin seemed to burst. She turned and saw the wings, at her back!

"You have but to concentrate on where you want to go, *Lizzybell*," Mihaela said. "Perhaps you would like to try flying out of the window?"

"I could not possibly!" Elizabeth exclaimed.

"Just fly across the bed then, if your faith is so frail."

Elizabeth focused on the other side of the bed and felt her feet lift off the floor. Startled, she looked down at the ground, losing her focus, which made her drop back to the floor with a loud thud.

From below, her mother's voice screeched, "My dear Mr. Bennet, what was that sound? Are the French coming? I'm certain that it came from Lizzy's room! Oh my, have they come to kidnap her?" Then a succession of rapid footfalls was heard, ascending the stairs.

The higher-level angel stiffened in alarm and disappeared.

"Wait! What about my wings?" Elizabeth hissed in agitation.

"Roll right, left and right and chant '*Artful and Ample, I am just a normal angel.* '"

"Silly chants!" Elizabeth muttered.

The fading voice of Michael warned, "Do not ridicule our angel's business or you may be punished." Then his tone softened, "If you should need me urgently, use the *petna* and write my name."

With that, the angel was gone. Elizabeth barely managed to murmur the incantation in time to hide her wings before Jane arrived to knock anxiously on the door. Responding, Elizabeth calmed her by telling her that she had simply fallen off the bed accidentally.

The next morning, Jane was invited to spend the day at Netherfield. Unfortunately, she fell ill after riding over in a storm, as per her mother's scheming instruction. Elizabeth visited her there on the second day and was invited to stay on. She did not give Mr. Darcy too much of a thought, as she was occupied with Jane's illness. But the same could not be said of the gentleman.

CHAPTER THREE

At first, Mr. Darcy believed that Miss Elizabeth Bennet was not so handsome as her elder sister and some of the beauties of his acquaintance in London. But her engaging and playful manner with everyone she encountered soon captured his attention.

After listening to some of her conversation with others, he conceded that she was witty, intelligent and well-read, a refreshing change from the fawning females of the ton.

Soon, he also had to admit that he found her figure light and pleasing, her sparkling eyes exceptionally fine. But the encounter at Sir William's left him in fear of his own desire. One minute, he was simply talking to her. Then she gave him the brightest smile he had ever seen, and it took his breath away. This was the first time she had talked with him directly and given him her full attention. He took in her bright countenance hungrily, his gaze wandering covertly down her alluring form, though he pretended not to look at her.

In another minute, as any red blooded man would do, he began to fantasise about how she might look, disrobed. He was particularly attracted to her generous bosom, which seemed to push dangerously close to spilling out from the low-cut décolleté of her yellow gown's thin muslin.

He often wondered why society's strictures should be so harsh on men. *How can I declare love and marriage to a woman if I am not first allowed some liberties? What if she cannot make me desire her? How can we create an heir together? So far, I have not found a woman in the ton who can challenge me on an intellectual level and yet make me desire her as well. If I found such a woman, one to whom I wished to declare myself, I would not be satisfied with simply holding her hand. I would want to admire more of her, to verify my desire.*

Mr. Darcy was thinking how happy he would be if society allowed such liberties – and, more specifically, how very much he would enjoy the sight of her naked form.

Not a second after this scandalous thought, Miss Elizabeth tipped her glass and wet the muslin of her bodice right in front of him. He swallowed hard as he took in the bewitching picture it created of her breasts. He had gotten his wish, but his balance was greatly disturbed in the process. Why had it happen as he wished? Had he blurted out his thought unconsciously, and had she then done it for his sake? But he did not *think* he had spoken his outrageous wish aloud. What had transpired must have happened purely by accident.

Now the woman was staying a few rooms away. *I must reframe from wayward thinking*, he told himself firmly. *I do not want any more such accidents to occur...do I?*

Because she was so busy caring for her sister, the first day of Elizabeth's stay passed uneventfully for him. He could not help admiring her dedication and loving nature. On the second day, she joined the Netherfield party at dinner and challenged him about the definition of an accomplished lady.

Did he say too much by declaring reading to be one of the characteristics he considered essential for a true lady? With her intelligence, she would be capable of deducing his admiration easily. He decided to be more careful in future.

Then her mother and younger sisters came to visit Miss Bennet the next morning. When Elizabeth defended him against her mother's silly remarks, Mr. Darcy believed she detected his fondness of her. And he could not prevent himself from asking her to dance a reel with him that night, even though she tried to make fun of him on account of the rigid notions about friendship that he had expressed to Mr. Bingley earlier in the day.

Surprised by her refusal to dance with him, he felt a sense of indignation. Rarely willing to dance on public occasions, he thought she should have felt honoured by his application. Her disinclination to dance outraged him. But the sweet way she turned him down made him believe that, at heart, she intended to flirt rather than offend. When he drifted off to sleep that night, a complacent smile adorned his face.

***

Relieved by the progress of Jane's recovery, Elizabeth prepared to retire. As she changed into her nightgown, she suddenly heard a 'call' from Mr. Darcy. She was startled, for it was the first time she had 'heard' her ward in her mind, 'asking' for her.

What should I do? She debated her options, but Mr. Darcy seemed most insistent in his demand, and so she opened the door and peered out into the corridor. It was silent and deserted.

Miss Bennet! His voice rang in her ears again.

Yes, I am coming! Compelled, she slipped out of her room, neglecting to pull on her robe. With almost military precision, she strode down the hallway and found his room without problem. But when she tried the door, it was locked. She had to detour and enter quietly through the servant's entrance.

In the dim moonlight, she could see that his shirt gaped open, as sweat dampened his brows and chest. His breathing was agitated, and hers became shallow upon her observation of his muscular physique; after all, as a maiden, she had never beheld such a manly vision.

She prodded his shoulder, waking him from what she thought a nightmare, hoping against hope that he would not question her presence in his room. When his eyes slowly opened, she braced herself to leave. But he bolted up, clinging to her hand, preventing her departure, and his eyes were fixed on hers in the moonlit room.

"You came!" he murmured, as if disbelieving the vision before him.

Astounded at being held fast by this half-dressed man in his dark chamber, she swallowed with difficulty and replied, as calmly as she could, reminding herself that she was an angel, not a mere woman on Earth. "You asked for me."

"Yes, I wanted to dance with you." He nodded his head and continued, "I wanted to share a waltz with you."

Eyes widening, Elizabeth tried again to back away but he rose smoothly from the bed and slipped his other hand around her waist, swirling her with him into the pattern of the dance. Her heart skipped a beat, and her entire body tingled in response to his closeness. The tips of her breasts brushed his chest, and her thinly clad belly registered the iron length of his bulge, hard and hot. His musky scent flooded her nostrils.

Elizabeth drew in fast deep breaths. When she opened her mouth to protest, he lowered his head and captured her lips in a heated kiss. In the next moment, his limbs abandoned all pretence of the dance and wrapped around her tightly, as if trying to impress his shape into her form, his hips moving rhythmically against her. His tongue thrust into her half-open mouth, tasting her, while his hands slid down to cup her buttocks, drawing her even closer.

Elizabeth had never felt such a mixture of sensations in her body. Blood rioted in her veins. Both her mouth and apex were hot and wet with desire, and she could not suppress the trembling that radiated from her core. She felt as if she were rising from the ground, flying to heaven.

...tap-tap...

The sound of someone knocking on the door shattered their heated embrace, driving them apart. Mr. Darcy whirled to face the intrusive sound's source and, stumbling, tumbled onto the bed. Elizabeth froze for a mere second before dashing for the servant's entrance.

...tap-tap...

He twisted to look after her retreating form as it faded in the darkness. "Wait!"

"Mr. Darcy!" The voice of Miss Bingley drew his attention away. When he looked again, the vision from his dream was gone.

He rubbed his eyes and swore under his breath, "Damn you for disturbing my sweet dream!" Then he rose and made his way slowly to the door. "Yes, Miss Bingley?" he responded without opening it.

"Mr. Darcy, I heard Charles mention that you had a headache, so I have brought young Margaret here to serve you some herbal tea," she said charmingly through the oaken panel.

"Thank you, Miss Bingley, but I am afraid you were misinformed. I am quite well and have no need of herbal tea. It is late, and I have already dressed for sleep. Thank you, Margaret," he said crisply, "and good night to you both."

"Oh!" He heard her stamp her foot in vexation and then stalk away in a huff. Shaking the lock to make sure it was well in place, he wondered if she had really brought a maid with her.

When all was peaceful once again, he walked back to the bed slowly. Peering through the moonlight, he surveyed the room for any sign of Miss Bennet. But there was not a trace. *Did I just dream of dancing a waltz with her? It cannot have been just a dream! I still feel hot and aroused...*

He lay down on the bed and closed his eyes, grimly amused at his own expense to discover than he now possessed the headache which he had just disavowed so firmly to Miss Bingley.

***

The next morning when Mr. Darcy awoke, he could still recall keenly the delicious taste of Elizabeth's mouth, and the sinuous generosity of her curves. He decided that it was one of the sweetest dreams he had ever had. Buoyed by his crystalline memories of it, he set out on a walk, intent on savouring the feeling.

Unfortunately, Miss Bingley saw him and insisted on joining him. She had somehow learned about his admiration of Miss Bennet's fine eyes at Sir William's gathering, and had been making fun of the country Miss ever since. Her constant mocking chatter about his future felicity with Elizabeth annoyed him more with each step he took.

When he and his disagreeable companion encountered the centre of his dream with Mrs. Hurst at the narrow lane, he was afraid that Elizabeth might have overheard Miss Bingley's latest thoughtless remarks. It seemed to him that Elizabeth appeared a bit flustered upon first seeing him but she recovered quickly. When Mrs. Hurst took Mr. Darcy's free arm, Elizabeth waved them all goodbye with her usual gaiety.

After dinner, Miss Bingley drew him into commenting on Elizabeth and her figures. When Elizabeth herself joined the debate, he found that he enjoyed the challenging discussion with the country Miss, so much so that he was afraid he had betrayed his interest to her again. As a result, he felt guiltily relieved upon learning that the two Miss Bennets would be leaving Netherfield the day after the next. He was determined to concentrate on more boring things, such as Miss Bingley's chatter, when he retired that night.

As he might have expected, that gave him a nightmare instead.

***

By the next afternoon, he was sitting alone in a dark corner of the library of Netherfield, reading a book entitled "The Peach" by A Titled Man. He had taken up the book from Bingley's family collection, thinking it would be a dull agricultural text. To his exasperation, he soon found that it was a novel about an attractive young gentlewoman's passionate initiation into adulthood by a beau.

The unnamed author, whether a man or a woman, used a great deal of symbolism to describe the sensual and erotic experience of the innocent maiden in question. Darcy told himself to put the book down, once he discovered what it was truly about. But the order was in vain. He could not seem to stop reading, not least because the name of the young woman in the book happened to be Elizabeth. It intrigued him that she was as impertinent and alluring as his Miss Elizabeth Bennet...

He uttered damnation when he reached the point where the young beau discovered Elizabeth in a small hut in the wood. Darcy closed his eyes and imagined himself as the beau, re-living what he had just read.

...I was soaked through, due to a sudden downpour and so I stripped myself to the skin in an abandoned hut deep in the wood. I had scarcely started a fire to dry my clothes when the impertinent Elizabeth came dashing in. She was wet through, as well. Little impeded by the thin, drenched muslin, my gaze travelled along her captivating mountains and valleys.

I finally recovered my manners and took up my shirt to cover the cucumber. When I saw that her fine eyes were drifting over my angles and planes with keen interest, I told her she was out of line. She replied archly that she did not see anything spectacular.

Angry and tempted, I quite forgot myself and pressed her against the hard oak door, drawing down the bodice of her dress to bare her cherries. My lips enjoyed the feast. She was willing and responsive, moving her form in a manner designed to entice me.

Then I pulled up her skirts and knelt before her, parting her supple thighs to admire her peach, the lips of which were red and swollen. I passed one of her slender legs over my shoulder and ran my eager tongue along the opening, savouring its sweet nectar. Nearly overcome, I employed my fingers to caress the lush golden flesh. She was eager and passionate, urging me on with sounds of endearment and encouragement.

After endless moments of worshiping her with my mouth and hands, I finally stood up and devoured the maidenly fruit fervently, with all my body and soul.

Legends from the Orient claim that such fruit makes men immortal. It may well be so. I must confess I felt I died a thousand times and reached heaven after feasting on her peach.

Mr. Darcy felt seriously hot and distressed after reading the text. Coupled with the restless night before, he soon fell asleep in the library.

***

Elizabeth had been shocked by Mr. Darcy's passionate kisses and caresses the other night. Arriving back at her bedchamber safely, she had wanted to call for Michael to appear immediately. She wanted answers! Was it the divine intent that she be 'used' by her ward in such a way? Were not angels supposed to be sacred? What dignity could she retain? But she did not have the magic quill with her; it was at home, locked safely in its drawer, and so she had little recourse but to throw herself into a fitful sleep, hoping Mr. Darcy would not ask for her again during her stay in Netherfield.

To her immense relieve, she passed a peaceful remainder of the night, as well as the next. But when she walked into the library on the day afterwards, she espied Mr. Darcy asleep in a chair, tucked away deep in a corner near the last shelf. He looked exhausted. His head rested at an awkward angle, his hair disheveled, his limbs sprawled.

She shook her head and thought, *Poor man! What has left him so worn out?* She walked two steps near him, aching to smooth the hair from his forehead, but thought better of it. However, as she turned to leave, he called out, "Elizabeth!"

She froze and sensed him coming near to her. His muscular arms encircled her waist, and he rested his chin lightly upon the top of her head. "Do not leave me," he said breathlessly. "I want you so!"

Torn, she told herself that she ought to struggle, and so she tried, but he took her movement as a welcoming sign. Lowering his head, he suckled her earlobe, his hands wandering up to cup her breasts.

She gasped and put her hands over his, trying to prevent his disturbing ministration, but he simply turned his palms to capture hers, sliding them over her bosom.

She had never stroked herself in such a manner before. Her hands felt scorched on both sides, by his hands and her own breasts. Her nipples hardened, her breathing grew painfully quick and shallow, and a traitorous wetness gathered at the juncture of her thighs.

As if sensing the weakness in her legs, he turned her around and placed her in the chair he had just vacated. Kneeling before her, he took her face in his hands and kissed her ardently.

Lost for words, she could only open her mouth to gasp for air. He took the opportunity to thrust his tongue into her mouth. The inside of her mouth was exactly as he remembered, sweet, soft and tender. Her tiny, clever tongue dueled with his in the most teasing, pleasing manner.

He wanted the dream never to end. His hands abandoned her face and smoothed downward, over her shoulders, drawing the sleeves and bodice down in the process. His large hands palmed the firmness of her twin peaks with fierce possessiveness, kneading and squeezing.

Elizabeth whimpered as he intimately aroused her mouth and caressed her bosom. But he took pity on her and drew the kiss to a reluctant close. Bereft of it, she panted, pushing her breasts into his demanding hands involuntarily.

His mouth did not rest for long. Moving down her neck, his hot lips trailed a wet journey that did not stop until it arrived at one of her nipples. While his teeth engaged in nipping and teasing at her creamy mound and its rosy peak, his fingers moved to gather the hem of her day dress.

Moaning softly, she arched and squirmed on the chair, with the result that he was able to gather the skirt of her dress and raise it to her waist, baring her supple thighs and lush bush as she tugged at his hair with frenzied fingers before collapsing in a near-swoon.

As she fell back into the chair's embrace, he stopped his worship of her chest and sat back on his heels, peering at her in concern.

The sight of her totally undid him.

She lay limp, her beautiful bosom exposed, nipples standing tall and hard, her legs slightly parted, allowing him a glimpse of the damp curls of her womanhood. Darcy's blood pounded in his veins, and his arousal came full on.

Taking a deep breath, desperate for the dream to continue, he gently parted her thighs and then, when she did not protest, bent forward to use the tip of his tongue to caress her folds. Elizabeth, innocently inexperienced in any such exquisite adventure, arched her body up to meet his touch, her hands gripping frantically at the arms of the chair.

Sliding his hands beneath her firm buttocks, he positioned her maidenly body more optimally for his erotic exploration. Sliding and thrusting, his magical tongue sampled her boiling core, exploring until he found her secret pearl.

Elizabeth was helpless to control her moans, which rose to a maddened, fevered pitch as he slid her legs over his shoulders, baring her more widely and deeply for his ardent ministration, until at last, driven beyond endurance, she screamed out in ecstasy and reached heaven.

Savouring the delicate taste of her that lingered upon his tongue, he breathed in her sexy scent and marveled at the convulsions that racked her innermost muscles, violent at first, then fading gradually away like echoing rumours of the delight that had just come to pass. For a long moment more, he gazed upon her, trying to commit the entrancing sight to memory. Then, overcome, he slumped to the floor in a stupor of exhaustion.

CHAPTER FOUR

Elizabeth's consciousness slowly returned from the cloud of passion where it had stranded her. As glorious as the encounter had been, she could not believe, in its aftermath, that she had abandoned years of proper upbringing and allowed him to kiss her in that most wanton and intimate of ways.

Amazed and bewildered by the incredible intimacy of the act, she could not understand her willingness to surrender her body to a man she believed to be arrogant and conceited. Why had it happened? Why had she been assigned to be his angel?

Cautiously, she raised herself from the chair, tidied her clothes as best she could, and gazed down at him. He lay sprawled on the floor at her feet, eyes closed, looking exhausted... Realisation struck her: he had fallen asleep. Insufferable man! How could he slumber on the library floor, just like that?

She stood up, debating what she should do. She supposed she could leave him...but what if Miss Bingley found him like this? Well then, should she stay by his side, in her role of guardian angel? Perhaps...but how could she face him after what they had done?

In the end, she left the room, closing the door with a loud, intentional slam, then waited at the corner where the hallway turned, to see if he had awoken.

Shortly afterwards, she had the satisfaction of watching him leave the library and head upstairs to his room. She could scarcely wait to leave Netherfield the next day, after church. She just needed to survive the dinner and the night.

To her relief, Mr. Darcy did not attend the dinner, citing an urgent matter that required his attention. When she retired to bed for the night, she closed the windows and all the doors, using chairs to block them, all to prevent herself from leaving the room.

Luckily, she received no 'call' from her ward that night. The next day, she returned home safely, without the embarrassment of setting eyes on him again. As soon as she was securely locked within her own room at Longbourn, she unlocked the drawer and hastened to write Mihaela's name with the *petna*. She needed answers, immediately!

Nothing happened.

Blast the woman, where is she? Elizabeth waited for another minute, then wrote: *Michael, the Lost Angel Commissioner.*

A few moments later, he appeared.

"What is it, *Lizzybell*?" Michael asked impatiently. "I am very busy seeking another lost angel."

"I need answers!" Elizabeth demanded.

"Concerning what?"

She felt a hot blush rise in her cheeks. "Are you not supposed to know everything that happens?"

"I am an angel only, I am not *Zenobie*." He raised his brows. "Your face is all red. This must be a woman matter!" He swiftly turned into Mihaela. "Now, tell me."

Elizabeth took a deep breath and said, "He...Mr. Darcy...was...ungentlemanly."

"Ungentlemanly?" Mihaela's brow furrowed. "He was rude to you? Why did you need me for a matter such as that? Simply teach him some manners."

"No!" Elizabeth exclaimed, embarrassed and exasperated "He kissed me and...you know..."

"I know what?"

"You know!" Elizabeth insisted, flustered, "You are a man! You must know. He took...advantage...."

"Oh. That." Mihaela tilted her head, eyeing Elizabeth. "And what is wrong with that?"

"What is wrong?" Elizabeth exclaimed, "I am a gentlewoman! I am supposed to remain virtuous."

"*Himins* is more liberal about such matters. You may bed other angels whenever you like."

Elizabeth sat down heavily on the bed. "Have I done that before? I mean, been intimate with other angels?"

"Actually, no, you have not, since you dropped from *Himins* when you were young."

She sighed with relief. "But Mr. Darcy is my ward! *Himins* allows that, too?"

"Yes, that is possible...although, in your case, it is more likely because of your past neglect of your duty."

"Neglect of my duty!" Elizabeth stood up angrily. "How was I to know about my duty if I did not even know I was an angel!"

Mihaela shrugged, avoiding her gaze.

"I think *you* neglected *your* duty!" Elizabeth accused. "You did not find me until now."

"I have a quota that requires me to find so many angels a year. I fulfill my duties, every year, quite conscientiously." The Commissioner shook her head. "Unfortunately, mishaps happen from time to time. Your case is on a queue and has been dealt with accordingly."

"So we poor level-six angels are left to provide reparation for events that occur due to mishaps?" Elizabeth was furious. "That is so unfair!"

"Mr. Darcy has been left without a guardian angel since he turned eight," Mihaela said. "If he wants you in that way, then it is your duty to bow to his demands. For that matter, what is the hardship? He is quite fine-looking. Did he not please you?"

"No ... yes ... but he is arrogant," Elizabeth's face turned bright red. "Why am I assigned to someone I do not respect?"

"We cannot always like what we are called to do," the Commissioner said. "In your case, I advise you to be thankful that he is handsome and virile, and that he is capable of pleasing you. If you do not wish to be intimate with him, then do not be near him any more often than is necessary. Or I suppose, if you wish, you could tell him the truth of your identity and ask him to mind his lustful thoughts. "

Elizabeth gaped. "He will think me insane."

"Show him your wings, and he will have no choice but to believe you," Mihaela reasoned. "But to be fair, I doubt that he can restrict his passionate thoughts. Men commonly think about sex all the time. It is their nature."

Elizabeth covered her flaming cheeks, then looked up, shocked by a sudden dire thought. "Will I be with child?" she asked, not entirely sure what the consequences of his intimate kisses might be.

"Oh, you need not worry about that," Mihaela said airily. "Guardian angels cannot become pregnant."

Elizabeth's eyes widened in distress. So then, not only would she soon lose the family she had known for the past twenty years, she was also destined never to have children of her own. She, who had always wanted to marry for the deepest of love and secretly wanted to have many children. How cruel!

"Well then, if you have no more questions," the angel said, "I shall get on with my search." She then disappeared in a puff of smoke.

Sagging down onto the bed again, Elizabeth swallowed back the rest of her questions. *What is the point in asking her when I may be going back to Himins, or when she plans to teach me more angelic skills? The place seems only to contain immortals with morals totally at odds with society as I know it here on Earth. With all of these endless rules and obligations, I do not want to become a real angel a single day before I must.*

Resting on the bed, she relived the events that had transpired at Netherfield. *Was I really helpless to deny Mr. Darcy's advance? In truth, I did not even try. What has happened to me? How could I be seduced by his kisses and outrageous caresses?*

More importantly, why should he want me? With his distant air, he seemed always before to look upon me with censure. He must be a scoundrel, to have the upbringing and countenance of a gentleman but the character of a rake.

He trifled with me as a country maiden and did not even bother to see me off. He only wanted me for that moment, with no regard to my situation or virtue.

I hate him! I would refuse to protect him, even if he was the last man in the world! He deserves to have trials and tribulations in his life, if he continues to behave in this most ungentlemanly manner.

Unhappy and vengeful, Elizabeth was in no mood to welcome the distant cousin who thereafter descended upon Longbourn. And she liked Mr. Collins no better when she learned that he had come to visit his long-lost relations with the firm intention of marrying one of the Bennet sisters, as suggested by his patroness, Lady Catherine de Bourgh.

Although her mother would love to see any one of her daughters become the future mistress of Longbourn, even she did not encourage him to pursue any one of them in particular, as he seemed a very silly sort of man. However, he soon seemed set upon having either Jane or Elizabeth.

A vain man who clearly felt his own importance after becoming the grand lady's clergyman, Mr. Collins appeared convinced that he would be an exceptional catch for any of his poor cousins. From the first, he surveyed them, one and all, in a condescending attitude. The way the man showed his preference for Jane and Elizabeth even made their mother cringe. But Mr. Bennet did not come to the rescue. It amused him to observe Mr. Collins's awkward pursuit of his daughters.

Today, Elizabeth's father appeared to have had enough of their fair cousin, and so, when the young ladies set out to walk to Meryton, the little town closest to their home, he encouraged Mr. Collins to leave the house and accompany them.

Elizabeth was disappointed to see that her father treasured his peace, quiet and sanity more than his daughters'. She sighed, feeling let down by all the men in her life.

When they arrived at Meryton, Captain Denny, an officer whom they had known before, introduced them to a new friend, a Mr. George Wickham. Tall and muscularly built, the new arrival had curly dark-brown hair and a pleasant manner.

"So, you will be joining the army, too?" Lydia asked, smiling with patent interest. "And will you be encamping here, like Captain Denny?"

"Indeed, Miss Lydia!" Wickham beamed, and continued, "I shall be most honoured to serve our country."

"Oh, we love to have more young men in Meryton," she said, "to help protect us, of course."

Elizabeth rolled her eyes at her youngest sister's crude fashion in flirting with a stranger. Turned her head away from the pair, she was startled to catch sight of Mr. Darcy riding on a magnificent white horse, accompanied by Mr. Bingley and heading directly towards them.

She panicked and wanted to leave immediately, but Mr. Bingley enquired after Jane's health when he approached. Mr. Collins hovered around the pair with impatience, and Elizabeth decided to stay. Drawing a steadying breath, she was about to greet Mr. Darcy when he and Mr. Wickham exchanged the strangest of look. One of the men turned red, the other white.

Mr. Wickham tipped his hat. The gentleman on horseback rode on, without taking his leave of Mr. Bingley or the Bennet sisters. Not long after, Mr. Bingley also took his leave.

Lydia invited Wickham to their aunt's gathering in the afternoon.

In some confusion, Elizabeth thought about the strange greeting that Mr. Wickham had exchanged with her ward. As a result, when he sat down beside her at the home of Aunt Philips and started a conversation, she was totally unprepared for the topic of discussion that he chose.

"So, you are *Lizzybell* the angel!" he said in a low voice, and flashed her a sly wink.

She opened her mouth but did not know how to reply. Had he somehow overheard Mihaela talking to her on some occasions? She could not think of how that could possibly be true.

"How… did you know?" she asked in consternation.

"Because I am like you." He raised his eyebrows with a smirk and continued, "*PickyWickly*, another fallen angel here, at your service!"

Upon hearing such a declaration, she nearly dropped her cup of tea. As she strove to gather her wits, she became most curious. "How is that you know about me but I knew nothing about you?"

"Michael is an overworked Commissioner," he said sweetly, "I provided him a few bottles of wine to help him relax."

"You got him drunk!" she flashed with anger. Of course – another disappointing man. "Did he tell you other things about me?"

"Why such fire, my dear?" he continued, "Do relax. He only told me that you are a level-six guardian angel who fell to Earth sometime after I did. He did not disclose the identity of your ward, or what you have been doing with him or her. He said his angelic memory only allowed him to handle details of a case when he was talking with that particular fallen angel."

It is lucky for me that Michael's memory is thus limited, she reflected. *I would not want this PickyWickly to know about what Mr. Darcy and I had done.*

"So then, who *is* your ward?" he asked.

"That, sir, is none of your business!"

"Now, now, I am only being friendly," he said with a mischievous twinkle in his eye, "as we are two uniquely lonely souls on this lowly world."

Given how handsome and charming he appeared, she believed she could have found in him a nice friend. But she was particularly wary of men at the moment, and so she proceeded carefully. "I do not wish to talk about myself, but you may tell me your story, if you are so inclined."

"Of course, my sweet." He smiled. "According to Michael, I am a level-seven angel."

"The lowest …" she murmured thoughtfully.

"Yes, I know, I am the lowest kind," he said with his hand on his heart, adopting an injured expression. "But I am different from you, for I am not a guardian angel."

"There are other kinds of angels?"

"Indeed, just as Michael is a Lost Angel Commissioner."

"Well, then, what is your duty?"

"I am a tempting angel," he said proudly, "responsible for tempting men and women to commit sin."

"What?!" She was flabbergasted. "*Himins* is crazy!"

"Actually, I find it quite marvelous. It explains all of my urges to gamble and drink with friends." He winked. "And, of course, to trifle with women."

Does he know about Mr. Darcy ... trifling with me? Indeed, did he tempt Mr. Darcy into doing so? I am going to be sick!

As if reading her thoughts, he asked, "How long have you known Darcy?"

"Only a month or so," She replied, trying to sound nonchalant. "And you?"

"Actually, I grew up at Pemberley with him."

She was astonished. "So he is one of the friends with whom you gamble and drink?"

"Well, we used to be good friends when we were young." He shook his head. "My father was his father's steward. But he changed. You saw our greeting, this morning. I wager he did not wish to see me at all."

"Whyever should that be true?"

"I think he was jealous of his father's attentions to me."

"He is so narrow-minded?" she was curious about this and wanted to encourage Mr. Wickham to tell more. "He seems like a gentleman to me."

"His father bestowed a living on me in his will," he said, then added grimly, "but Darcy denied it to me when the time came."

"But that is horrible!" she exclaimed. "Did you go to the authority to report him?"

"He is rich," Wickham said, shaking his head. "What would be the point? But, of course, I know now why I could not be a clergyman. It would be scandalous for a tempting angel to preach for morality and chastity," he observed with a cunning smile.

Upon hearing such a frank admission, she flinched and remained silent.

Mr. Wickham, not seeming to notice her discomfort, pushed on. "May I tempt you too?" He grinned and whispered, "I have learned that *Himins* is very liberal about bedding our fellow angels, and you do have the most gorgeous bosom."

Suppressing the urge to strike his face, Elizabeth stood up abruptly and left the immoral angel behind.

**

In the next few days, she did not use the *petna* at all, separating herself from the intimidating act of learning about more angelic duties, telling herself that she had lost interest in it. The house was in chaos anyway. Her mother's constant nervous condition created a frenzy in the house by her insistence upon the best lace, the best gowns and the best dance steps for her daughters as they prepared for the Netherfield Ball. Mr. Collins's silly presence added fuel to the fire, as he insisted upon dancing two sets each with the two eldest sisters.

Jane was already promised to Mr. Bingley for the first two sets. Elizabeth was less fortunate, and therefore could not in all honesty refuse her cousin. The misfortune did, at least, prevent her mind from drifting back quite so often to Mr. Darcy.

She breathed a sigh of relief when she encountered neither Mr. Darcy nor Mr. Wickham at the beginning of the ball. However, after suffering the first two sets of dancing with Mr. Collins, she was suddenly approached by Mr. Darcy. Taken unaware, she agreed to dance with him.

When he took her hand and led her to the dance floor, it attracted a great deal of attention. The rich gentleman had not danced with any local woman in the past month that he had been in residence in Hertfordshire. Gossip flew immediately. Had he taken a fancy to Miss Elizabeth? She had stayed at Netherfield for several days. Could they be more than just acquaintances?

If Elizabeth had heard the gossip, she would have died of embarrassment. But her heart was beating fast as she felt her whole body tremble with heightened sensation. *Am I reliving the time of waltzing with him?* She asked herself shakily.

She gazed up at him, silently willing him to confess and apologise for his breach of propriety. No such word came. He remained silent and intense while they danced, staring down at her with a hazy, dazed expression.

In the end, she could stand the silence no longer, and said, "I hope you are well, sir, since I last saw you at Meryton."

His countenance turned even graver, and he replied, "I am well. Do you walk there often?"

"Yes, our mother encourages us to exercise," she said, and decided in that moment to attempt to learn more about his relationship with the licentious fallen angel. "We first made Mr. Wickham's acquaintance on the day that you were there. He tells me that the two of you grew up together."

"Yes, his father was a fine man," Mr. Darcy said through gritted teeth.

Elizabeth raised her eyebrows. "And his son?"

"He has charming manners that make him popular with his friends," he said, and added as an after thought, "How long he can keep them may well be another matter."

"He is unfortunate to have lost your friendship." She wondered if he would confess to having denied Mr. Wickham's living.

He drew a deep breath and replied coldly, "One person's misfortune is sometimes another's luck."

What an insufferable man! He had no mercy on people not from his social sphere. "Do you admit to reducing him to his present poverty?" she asked, unable to disguise her outrage.

"I can only confirm that he has charming manners that can cause unsuspecting, simple women to fall for him," he retorted in a low voice, his eyes flashing in anger.

"I am no simple woman."

"And I am no villain."

"So you did not deny him the living left to him by your father?"

The music stopped at that moment. Mr. Darcy bowed and said, "My sympathy goes out to you, for having to listen to a story so unsubstantiated by facts." Then he turned and left her.

Elizabeth was furious. *So that is his opinion of me? That I am unsuspecting? Simple? Pitiful? And what of him? A rake! A scoundrel! But he will not be able to dismiss me so easily, once he knows that I am his angel.*

So decided, she walked forth with long strides, following him in the direction of the library.

As she took a turn into the long corridor, however, her vision suddenly turned to black. Someone had thrust a bag over her head, and then proceeded to pick her up and walk quickly, out! Elizabeth fought against her captor as best she could, with vigour and courage, but her screams were muffled by the encompassing bag, and her frantic kicks proved fruitless.

CHAPTER FIVE

In the library, Mr. Darcy opened a half-filled decanter of whisky and gulped down a large mouthful directly from it, not bothering with a glass. Enraged by Wickham's lies and Elizabeth's accusation, he attempted to drown his fury with the liquid.

This visit to Hertfordshire has proven to be worse than a waste of time.

He drank another mouthful of whisky and assessed the situation.

Georgiana was as despondent as before. Bingley did not set his mind to learning how to manage an estate, preferring rather to focus upon the smiles of the eldest Miss Bennet. Miss Bingley was even more annoying than she had been before, which was no small accomplishment. But, worst of all, he hated the way that he repeatedly lost control of his mind and emotions in the presence of Miss Elizabeth.

He raised the decanter to his mouth again.

How could a mature man of eight-and-twenty years dream of dancing a waltz with a maiden who left him hot and aroused? Worse yet, he had fallen asleep in broad daylight in

Bingley's library and experienced the most vivid dream of devouring the country Miss.

He needed the burning liquid. He gulped again.

The smell of sex and lavender in the room had been the telltale signs that it was more than a dream.

But how could that be possible? Whyever would she allow him to take such unconscionable liberties? Had he forced himself on her, in his dream-state? And yet he remembered her passionate responses, which belied the possibility that he had forced her beyond her inclinations. And, as further reassurance, Mr. Bennet had not arrived at Netherfield with a gun, demanding that he marry his daughter.

He began to think again that it must all have been a dream.

How disagreeable it had been, when he saw Wickham with her. The scoundrel! What was he doing here, in Hertfordshire?

Another taste of the whisky would wipe the rake's image away.

Was it his duty to warn Elizabeth ever more directly about Wickham?

Tonight, she had not sought his company. And she had seemed shocked when he asked her to dance. But when he held her hands and gazed at her, he was almost certain that he had danced with her before. He did not know how to raise the subject of the midnight waltz, let alone what might have happened in the library. Then she had spoken, accusing him of reducing Wickham's situation and behaving badly to his childhood friend.

Temper flared in Darcy's chest. He raised the decanter again, but it was empty. He threw it against the fireplace, smashing it to pieces, but the violence brought him no pleasure and no relief. With head throbbing, he walked to the window and flung it open, taking deep breaths of the cool night air.

Then he heard a muffled cry, and spotted a wisp of white disappearing in the wood. It looked for all the world like a woman, flung struggling over the shoulder of her captor.

Damnation! I do not need this now! Mr. Darcy thought, wishing that he could simply shut the window and seek out another decanter of spirits with which to drown his anger. But his gentlemanly upbringing forced him instead, to dash out of the library and seek the nearest door opening onto the woods at the back of the house.

He ran as quickly as he could and was rewarded, first by a renewed glimpse of white, and then as he emerged from a copse of trees, by a clear sight of the couple. They had taken shelter by an outcropping of rocks, and he clearly heard the woman scream.

As he rounded the rock, he was astonished to see Miss Elizabeth using a tree branch to smite Wickham's head repeatedly.

"Stop! You are mad!" Wickham screeched, attempting to protect his head with his hands. "I just want to better acquaint with you. We are the same kind. Why struggle?"

"Rake!" she screamed.

Wickham spotted Darcy and begged for help. "Darcy, stop her! She will kill me."

Upon hearing Mr. Darcy's name and seeing him there, all of the strength deserted Elizabeth, and she lowered the hefty branch to her side. Wickham took advantage of her unguarded moment to run away into the trees without a backward glance.

"Scoundrel!" Elizabeth yelled after him, brandishing the branch anew as if she intended to race after Wickham. "I shall kill you, you horrible man."

Darcy's eyes widened at her spirited exhibition of fire and temper. Wrapping his arms around her, he tried to draw her near. "Let him go, Miss Bennet," he urged as she continued to struggle, for he did not want her to be hurt.

"Let go of me!" She sniffed and pushed away from him. "You are drunk!" she accused, and struck him across the face with the branch.

"Ouch!" He let go of her and dropped to the ground, holding his face where the branch had struck him.

"Oh, my Lord!" Elizabeth exclaimed as she saw blood appear in the moonlight. She threw away the branch and crouched by his side. "I am so sorry, Mr. Darcy. I did not mean to injure you. I was just so overset – " Moving his hand aside, she took out her handkerchief and pressed it against his cheek.

The earlier angry words she had exchanged with him, her frightening kidnapping by Wickham, the struggle to free herself, and now the discovery that she had injured her ward was too much for Elizabeth. As Mr. Darcy scrambled up on one elbow, she wrapped her hands around his neck and burst out crying, carrying them both to the ground again.

He returned her embrace, gently smoothing her back as she cried her heart out, although his head had begun to pound. He closed his eyes, savouring her sweet smell and soft body.

By the time Elizabeth finally stopped sobbing, she discovered that Mr. Darcy had fallen asleep beneath her. Anger flared in her chest again. How could he sleep at such a time and place? They had been gone from the ball room for more than a quarter of an hour. They would need to return immediately or risk speculation about their whereabouts.

She shook his shoulders firmly but he did not move so much as an eyelash. *What can I do? Leave him here?*

Suddenly, lightening flashed in the sky followed by a loud clap of thunder. Elizabeth raised her gaze to the sky and bit her lip. Then resigned to her fate, she rolled her shoulders, left, right and left, and chanted *"Crosswind and Whirlwind, I trust Ventara the God of Wind."*

The base of her neck felt as if it might burst. And then it did, and her wings spread out.

Elizabeth stood up, concentrated on a tree not far from the rock, and felt her body lift off the ground as she flew there and landed safely.

With a deep sigh of relief, she flew back to Mr. Darcy's side, this time with more confidence. When she still could not rouse him, she crouched down besides him and, with as much strength as she could gather, gave a shout and pushed him to a sitting position from behind, with her hands wrapped around his chest.

"Come, Mr. Darcy," she panted. "You must help me or we shall both soon be drenched and risk getting sick. Stand up, please."

When drops of rain started to fall, they seemed to wake him from his stupor. He turned his head to peer at her and mumbled, "Wings?"

"Yes. I am your guardian angel." She pushed at him again. "You must stand up now."

"Silly," Mr. Darcy chuckled and turned his body so that he was braced on all fours on the ground. "Only Bing... has angel."

She groaned in frustration and stood up, wrapping her hands around his waist from behind. "Up!"

He stood up, wavering in a tipsy manner, bracing his hands on the boulder as rain started to fall harder. Elizabeth slipped around to his front and clasped her arms firmly around him. "Hold tight!" she entreated, closed her eyes, and thought about his bedchamber.

"Angel," he murmured in her ear. "You...smell of ...lavender." Then he stiffened in her grasp. "Holy Lord! We are...flying."

She wanted to tell him to shut up, but as soon as her attention drifted from visualising his bedchamber, she lost altitude. Her heart faltered in alarm.

"Crashing!" He wrapped himself around her like a python and muffled a cry of alarm against her shoulder. "Have you flown before, little angel? I do not...want to...die."

She blocked out his voice.

Concentrate. Concentrate.

Slowly, they regained altitude, higher, and then higher still. The rain and the wind struck like icy fingers at their faces and bodies. Finally, they flew to the open window of his bed chamber and landed safely within the room.

Mr. Darcy leaned against the wall by the window, still tightly enfolding her. "Again, angel. Higher. I want...to fly higher."

"Unhand me!" She pushed at him, "I must go back down to the ballroom before anyone notices that I have been absent."

As soon as he relaxed his hold, she turned to leave, but he grabbed part of her wing from behind. "So soft..." Bending his head on her wings, he grazed his cheek against the soft feathers.

A shivering tingle coursed through her entire body, leaving her hot and flustered. Her legs went weak as his damp breath, smelling of whisky, blew softly on her neck and ear from behind. With a low groan, he rubbed his body against her.

"Do not..." Before she could finish her sentence, she felt his arousal thrust against her bottom. The sensation was unbelievable, scorching and rock hard.

"Mmm," she moaned, and squirmed.

"Very...soft," he murmured, and licked the place where the wings joined the base of her neck.

She put her hands against the wall to prop up her weakening body, but her Herculean-like strength was gone.

She felt his hands steal around to stroke her bosom. She let her head drop back, allowing him to trace a string of kisses along her neck to her earlobe.

His hands worked magic, shaping her twin peaks through the thin, damp garment, reminding her of their previous intimate encounter.

Involuntarily, she reached to caress his body, angling her buttocks to press hungrily against his bulge.

While she was busy shaping her body to his, his hands moved down to gather handfuls of her dress, drawing the material higher and higher until he could cup the curve of her sex. At his touch, her legs gave way, and she slid, inch by inch, to her knees on the floor, her hands still pressed against the wall.

He followed her down, burying his face in her wings, parting her legs with his. Molding his large hands to the lush curve of her bottom, he murmured again, "Soft."

This time, when he rubbed his arousal against her from behind, her heart stopped beating for a second. She felt him grasp her thighs and part them more widely. Reaching around her, he sent his clever fingertips delving within her cleft as he pushed his body hypnotically against hers, imitating the act of union.

She gasped in ecstasy. He continued the movements, treasuring this new closeness to her. The sound of their moans was loud and grew steadily louder, punctuated by gasps, until Elizabeth shrieked, reaching her peak.

She shivered in the aftermath of her climax, and he turned her, drawing her down, parting her thighs, guiding her to straddle him. Reaching up, he caressed her breasts through the dampened muslin, his touches and pinches awakening desire in her once again.

"Ride, angel," he urged. "Ride..."

She braced her palms on his broad chest and began to slide her hips. Responding to his passionate calls, she rubbed her apex against the fabric that struggled to contain his bulge, riding him as she might struggle to tame a wild stallion. Forward and back, forward and back she travelled, her breath coming faster and faster as she raked her nails over the sleek shirt that covered his chest. His eyes gazed up at her gorgeous bosom as it loomed and gyrated above him. Inspired, he arched his body up to meet her, lunge for lunge, until his bulge erupted, staining his breeches with the flood of his ardour.

Mr. Darcy groaned in ecstasy, finally fully sated.

He had never been ridden by a woman before, and this one had driven him onward without mercy, totally exhausted him. As he fought to catch his breath, the volumes of alcohol he had consumed seemed to rampage through his veins and nostrils. His head grew irresistibly heavy, and he sank into a deep, whisky-induced slumber that bordered on unconsciousness.

***

Meanwhile, in the ballroom, it was time for supper, and the absence of both Mr. Darcy and Miss Elizabeth raised eyebrows and speculations.

Miss Bingley summoned Mr. Darcy's valet to ascertain his whereabouts. When Wharton arrived at his master's room, he was astonished to find Mr. Darcy drunk, asleep on the floor, his clothing stained and in disarray, his body smelling of lavender and sex.

He immediately set to cleaning up Mr. Darcy, then helped him into a nightgown. All the while, his master murmured a stream of nonsensical words.

Barely had Wharton completed the task of making Mr. Darcy neat and tidy, resting on the bed, before Miss Bingley knocked upon the door, with her brother in tow.

Wharton hurried to answer before her knocking could awaken Mr. Darcy.

"Did you find your master?" Miss Bingley demanded. "What took you so long?"

Gritting his teeth, Wharton bowed and replied calmly, "Mr. Darcy had imbibed a bit too much whisky and requested my assistance."

When Miss Bingley wanted to step inside to see Mr. Darcy for herself, Wharton prevented her advance and said, "Mr. Bingley, would you care to check on my master? If not, I think he should be left to rest."

With a scowl, Miss Bingley turned to her brother. "Check on him, Charles! He may need better attention than his servant can provide."

"Go down to the ball room, Caroline," Bingley told his sister, clearly registering Wharton's displeasure concerning the proprieties of the situation. "Wharton knows what is best for Darcy." He waited while she made her way reluctantly down the corridor and out of sight. Then he returned his attention to Wharton. "Now, let me see."

As Bingley approached, Darcy opened his eyes halfway and broke out in drowsy chuckles. "I have…an angel too, Bing…"

Bingley smiled down at him with genuine affection. "You are drunk, Darce. Go back to sleep."

"Guess…what we have…done," Darcy said, his eyelids drifting down.

"We?"

"My…angel…and I."

Wharton hovered anxiously. The room had clearly borne a woman's intimate scent when he first entered. Surely the master was not going to tell Mr. Bingley anything…indiscreet…?

"We flew." Darcy smiled. "My angel…took me… to fly."

Bingley shook his head and thanked Wharton. When he left Mr. Darcy's room, he found his disgruntled sister awaiting him at the turn of the hallway.

When they returned together to the assembled guests, they learned that Mr. Bennet and Miss Mary had left earlier, to check on Miss Elizabeth. According to Mrs. Bennet, her second daughter had been overcome by a headache earlier, and had gone home. Miss Elizabeth had left a note with the coachman, asking him only to entrust it to her father when an hour had passed, for fear of disrupting the family's enjoyment of the ball.

After Bingley confirmed Mr. Darcy's whereabouts, the general speculation concerning the disappearance of Mr. Darcy and Miss Elizabeth died down.

When Mr. Bennet arrived home, he found his second daughter sound asleep in her bed, where she had apparently been settled for quite some time.

***

Eyes closed, Elizabeth listened as her father crept out and closed the door of her bedchamber, only then permitting herself a sigh of relief.

She thought back over the evening's events with annoyance. Not long before, in the bedchamber at Netherfield, as she was first recovering from the passionate haze induced by Mr. Darcy's love-making, she had berated herself for again falling prey to her ward's charm and desires. Disentangling herself from Darcy's recumbent form, she had taken up a piece of paper from his desk and composed a letter for her father. Then, after gathering her concealing cloak and reticule, she had given the note to the coachman, hoping that her father would not question him. Finally, she had darted back to the woods and, safely out of sight, had begun to fly. The sweep of her wings enabled her to reach home, tidy up and pretend to be asleep within a quarter of an hour.

But now, when she tried to truly sleep, after her entire family had returned, she found that she could not, for her troubled thoughts would grant her no peace.

Why, when PickyWickly tried to kiss me, did I only feel revulsion? But with Mr. Darcy, I must confess, I wanted more of his kisses, as well as his touch. I acted like a wanton. Indeed, he made me scream with ecstasy and reach the heavens, time and again. Whatever am I to do? Would it not be best if he were simply to go away? Surely I could not be expected to fly all the way to London or Derbyshire to be with him, and so, at last, I might find some peace. But why, then, does the very thought of being separated from him bring me to the brink of desperate tears?

CHAPTER SIX

The next morning, Mrs. Bennet prevented Mr. Collins from asking Miss Elizabeth for a private audience, citing her daughter's headache of the night before. She was not, however, quick enough to forestall him from cornering Jane.

To Jane's consternation, the clergyman promptly asked for her hand in marriage, explaining his generosity in offering for her, thus saving her sisters and her from a destitute life should her father die suddenly.

Miss Bennet rejected him politely; nevertheless, Mr. Collins was offended. When he expressed a desire to reason with Mr. Bennet concerning the matter, the lady of the house dissuaded him, telling him that Mr. Bennet would not force any of his daughters to marry against their will.

Outraged by the ungratefulness of the Bennet women as a whole, he accepted Charlotte Lucas's invitation to her house for tea. Not many hours thereafter, he returned to inform the Bennets that he was engaged to be married, with Miss Maria Lucas.

The Bennet family felt sympathy for Miss Maria, to be married so young and to a self important silly man.

By the next day, however, it was the Bennet family who was receiving the sympathies of their Meryton neighbourhood. The two rich young men who had seemed to show such a keen interest in the two eldest Bennets left Hertfordshire suddenly.

The general population also pitied Mr. Darcy, whom misfortune seemed to befall whenever he was in their neighbourhood. Apparently Mr. Darcy had been taken ill, the night of the ball, and required the doctor's attention in town. Mr. Bingley was worried for his friend and, of course, left to accompany him.

Miss Bingley sent a letter to inform Miss Bennet that all their party was departing for town, as a result, and that they had no plan to return during the winter. She continued:

> *It is also good for Charles to meet with Mr. Darcy's sister. Miss Georgiana is so accomplished. Charles likes to listen to her singing. What a felicity it will be should a certain happy event occur!*
>
> *But I must not think about this at the moment. Mr. Darcy is in ill health. Charles, Miss Georgiana and I, most particularly, must see to his swift recovery. Miss Georgiana and her servants depend on my opinions, I am most humbly thankful for that as I care for her family exceedingly.*
>
> *It was great to make your acquaintance in Hertfordshire but I must say I shall be too busy to continue corresponding with you, with so much happening in town. But you can write any time.*
>
> *Your trusted friend,*
>
> *Miss Caroline Bingley*

"Arrogant woman!" Elizabeth murmured. "Who does she think she is? *I, most particularly, must see to his swift recovery!* She is nothing to him, compared to me."

In addition to worrying about Jane's low spirits upon learning of Mr. Bingley's interest in Miss Georgiana, Elizabeth was also distressed upon hearing about Mr. Darcy's illness.

Had he develop pneumonia after being caught in the rain? Had she failed in her duty yet again? Or had he gone away, as she had prayed, to spare her from yielding to his insatiable sexual desires?

She swore that she would not use her angelic *petna* again, and she reframed from asking for Mihaela. Not even *PickyWickly* was around. She had no recourse but to carry her vexation alone into the depth of winter.

Christmas brought her Aunt and Uncle Gardiner from London. Seeing the low spirit of their two favourite nieces, they invited Jane and Elizabeth to London after the festive holiday. Then, from London, Elizabeth would join Lydia in March to visit Hunsford, as a guest of the newly married Mrs. Maria Collins.

Elizabeth did not wish to go to London at first. She was concerned about being too near to Mr. Darcy. What if he called for her again? But her worries about his health continued to plague her. Jane had received no more letters from Miss Bingley, despite writing several to her, and so Elizabeth had no news of him. She wanted to be near him, to protect him from any and all misfortune.

With these two desires warring against each other within her mind, she packed her trunk and travelled to London, filled with equal measures of anticipation and dread.

***

Elizabeth regretted her decision to come to London the first day she arrived. True, she was happy to get away from the silly conversation of her younger sisters in Longbourn and indulge on her nieces and nephews in London. However, she was soon dismayed by the disturbing calls within her mind from Mr. Darcy that soon transpired. Not knowing where he lived, she could not respond to him, and that was just as well, for she was, of course, afraid to fly in London. What if someone were to see her?

She soon believed that he must not be sick at all because, at almost every hour of the day, she could 'hear' his ungentlemanly demands. He wanted to pinch her bottom in a busy room of people, to stroke her bosom in some secluded corner of a modiste's shop, or even ride naked with her on horseback in Hyde Park!

His thoughts left her agitated and totally distracted from whatever she was supposed to be doing at the time. Her uncle and aunt, as well as Jane, commented on her lack of concentration and stated their worry.

By night, matters grew much worse. Darcy would play out long moments of fantasy, with her at the centre stage. She 'heard' him wanting to devour her in the bath, washing her hair, massaging her neck and shoulders, and making her scream with ecstasy while sitting in the tub.

Or he would place her on the table in the bedchamber and make love to her in front of the big mirror, admiring the manner in which her voluptuous figure shivered and trembled under his ministrations.

Overcome on these nightly occasions, Elizabeth would follow Darcy's thoughts and caress her own body just as he directed, groping her breasts, pinching her nipples, cupping her sex and sliding a daring finger along her folds.

Blast the man! Did he not have a moment of pure thoughts? Must he drive her to climax every night – and not just once, but sometimes several times in a single night.

She hoped that she would not encounter the man in London. She would not know how to behave. But when a few weeks had passed and Jane announced her intention to call upon Miss Bingley, Elizabeth loyally accompanied her elder sister, however reluctant she might feel in the privacy of her own mind.

***

"My dear Miss Bennet," Miss Bingley exclaimed upon seeing Jane. "Why did you not tell me you were coming to London?"

"I sent you three letters," Jane said with confusion. "They must have gone astray."

"Such a bad postal service we have from Hertfordshire to London," her hostess continued, "I am so sorry I cannot receive your call for long. Louisa and I have an appointment with an herbal doctor and must leave now."

"Indeed, we hate to cause any inconvenience," Elizabeth was as eager to leave as Miss Bingley was to have them gone. She did not want to chance a meeting with Mr. Darcy at the Hurst townhouse. But as she and Jane stood to take their leave, two gentlemen and a woman came in.

"Caroline, I must..." Mr. Bingley stopped in mid-sentence as he beheld the lovely vision of Jane Bennet. "Miss Bennet! What a surprise to see you in London."

"Mr. Bingley." Jane curtsied. "It is good to see you again. I am sorry we came at an inopportune time. We are about to leave."

"Inopportune?" Mr. Bingley frowned and looked at his sister.

Miss Bingley explained, her lips thin with displeasure, "We were unaware of Miss Bennet and her sister's arrival in London, and their call was untimely. Louisa and I have an appointment which cannot be delayed."

"Then let us not detain you, Miss Bingley," Mr. Darcy said, speaking for the first time since entering the room. "If Bingley has no objection, perhaps my sister may act as the hostess."

He gestured to his sister. "Miss Bennet, Miss Elizabeth, may I have the honour of introducing my sister Georgiana. Georgiana, I had the privilege of making their acquaintance while I stayed with Mr. Bingley in Hertfordshire."

The ladies curtsied and Mr. Bingley gestured for them to sit. Seeing that the Darcys were intent on staying, Caroline abandoned her plan to force the Bennet sisters to leave. All that was left to her now was to control the damage of the chance encounter as best she could. She exclaimed, "My goodness, how foolish of me – I totally confused the date. The appointment with the herbal doctor is for tomorrow. Let us sit and have some refreshment."

"Are your parents in good health?" Mr. Bingley started the conversation, trying to engage Miss Bennet to talk. She had become silent upon first seeing Miss Darcy in Bingley's company. Given that young gentlewoman's elegant manner of dress and sweet voice and visage, Jane felt she herself had no attribute that could compare.

"They are well, thank you," she replied mildly, and tried not to focus on Bingley's eager expression. Turning instead to Mr. Darcy, she said, "I hope you have recovered from the illness that forced you to leave Hertfordshire so suddenly, Mr. Darcy."

"Were you not feeling well when you returned to London?" Georgiana asked her brother, looking confused and concerned.

Mr. Darcy blushed and stole a glance at Elizabeth, who had also been very quiet since the gentlemen arrived. Shaking his head, he said, "I did have a hang…headache when I left Netherfield, but I came back to London because of … some urgent business matters."

"So you were not ill?" Elizabeth sighed in relief. Angry over Miss Bingley's dubious actions and determined to expose her, she continued, "Miss Bingley was kind enough to send Jane the bad tidings, explaining that you had fallen ill and needed the attention of a doctor in town, and that Mr. Bingley, concerned, therefore accompanied you in the journey. She informed us that Mr. Bingley would be very busy with taking care of you, Mr. Darcy. The neighbourhood has been speculating about it, lamenting that misfortunes seem to befall you whenever you are in Hertfordshire."

Both Bingley and Darcy glared at Caroline. She laughed, colouring, and said, "Did I really write that? I fear you must have misunderstood me, my dear Jane."

"Yes, Caroline does like to jest," Bingley said, trying to diffuse the situation.

"Whenever you are in Hertfordshire?" Georgiana repeated, clearly startled. "You had been there before?"

Relieved by the change of subject, Caroline said, "Did you not know? Mr. Darcy had a carriage accident there, some ten years ago. Indeed, perhaps he should not go back there again. The place may be bad luck for him."

"Nonsense!" Bingley said, "It was Darcy who encouraged me to look at the estates around that area."

Everyone turned their gaze towards the tall gentleman, at Bingley's latest revelation. Darcy's face reddened slightly, but he said, "The accident was a serious one. But I was saved by a pretty little girl. After that, Sir William and the others treated my men and myself very well."

"A little girl?" Caroline was curious. "How very strange. Why have we not heard of this before?"

"I thought Sir William found you," Bingley added.

Mr. Darcy gazed at Elizabeth and said, "She helped me free my leg, which was trapped under the carriage. She had the most expressive eyes, and dark curly hair. I admired her courage and would have liked to make her acquaintance but she left without giving her name. Many Hertfordshire people are good people. That was why I recommended that you look there for an estate."

Elizabeth's heart was in turmoil. *He remembers and admired my courage? He thought Hertfordshire a good place to settle? And yet he was so haughty. I do not understand the man.*

"And you did not find out who she was, this time when you were there?" Georgiana asked.

He shook his head and continued to gaze at Elizabeth. She felt uncomfortable under his eyes.

"Perhaps we should leave now," she suggested to Jane. But her sister wanted to learn more about Miss Darcy and was therefore reluctant to leave.

It became clear that Mr. Bingley was equally disinclined to have the meeting end. He asked, "Would the two of you have time to stay for dinner? I know it is short notice but it has been quite a long few weeks since we have seen you. I would like to enquire more about the latest news from my neighbours."

Jane looked at her sister. But before the sisters could come to an agreement, Caroline interrupted, "Charles, you forget we are to dine … with the Harringtons tonight?"

"Are we?" Bingley said with annoyance and added under his breath. "Who the hell are the Harringtons?

"Miss Bennet and Miss Elizabeth," Mr. Darcy said, "I hope to enquire about the latest news from Hertfordshire as well. If you are not otherwise engaged, my sister and I would like to invite you and your aunt and uncle to Darcy House for dinner tonight. I assume you are staying with your uncle?"

Jane was surprised by the invitation, and Elizabeth wished above all things to find a way to get out of it, but Miss Darcy added eagerly, "We would be most honoured to have you tonight, Miss Bennet. We do not entertain much in London and I should very much like to know more about my brother's stay in your neighbourhood."

Seeing that the young lady was genuine in her invitation, Jane nodded and said, "We have no prior engagement, but we do need to check with our uncle and aunt for their permission."

"Of course," Mr. Darcy said. "Did you come with your uncle's coach or a hired one? Perhaps Mr. Bingley and I can see the two of you back, and I shall ask your aunt's permission, myself."

Seeing Mr. Darcy's eagerness, Caroline berated herself. Not only had she missed the chance of having dinner at the Darcy House, she left him to the arts and allurements of that upstart chit as well.

She had to do something. Standing, she said, "It is cold outside. Let me get some hot tea for you before you leave."

Then she abandoned the room in a rush, leaving everyone puzzled as to why she had not simply rung for a servant to carry out the task.

When she returned, she instructed the maid to serve the tea to Mr. Darcy first, then to Miss Darcy, her brother and Mrs. Hurst before serving the two Bennet sisters.

After everyone had finished their tea, Mr. Darcy was eager to go but Miss Bingley said, "Ah, Georgiana, I forgot I have a cover screen here that I need to show you. Pray give me a few moments. I shall be right back." She then left the room again before Miss Darcy could reply.

The guests looked after their hostess with varying degrees of exasperation, doing their best to chat on while they waited impatiently for her return. Before long, Mr. Darcy, his sister, Mr. Bingley and Mrs. Hurst were feeling quite sleepy, while the Bennet sisters were not feeling well at all. Jane and Elizabeth were both holding their stomachs, wincing with pain, by the time Miss Bingley returned.

"Oh my goodness, what happened?" she exclaimed.

"Excuse me, Miss Bingley." Elizabeth swayed to her feet and rushed from the drawing room to ask for direction for relief, with Jane on her heels.

With the Bennet sisters out of the room, Miss Bingley summoned the servants to help the remainder of the room's occupants to the guest and family chambers upstairs.

When Jane and Elizabeth finally felt better to return to the drawing room, they were summarily seen off by Miss Bingley. She told them that Mr. Darcy, also feeling suddenly unwell, was resting in a guest chamber and could not see to their departure but that he had left a message to cancel the night's dinner invitation, due to the sudden illness.

Elizabeth and Jane left the Hurst townhouse, deeply troubled. Elizabeth suspected foul play on the part of their hostess, while Jane was gravely disappointed. *But how could I intervene?* Elizabeth thought glumly. *Surely, Miss Bingley did not intend any harm to either Miss or Mr. Darcy...*

But not a few minutes into the carriage ride back to Cheapside, Elizabeth 'heard' Mr. Darcy's call: *I need you.*

What can I do? She bit her lip and thought. *Jane is with me. I cannot fly back to him now. It is still daylight. And yet how can I deny him?*

Her gaze searched the carriage wildly for a moment. Then she bowed over, her arms holding her stomach, and cried loudly, "Pray stop the carriage!"

Their uncle's coachman heard her and stopped immediately.

"What is happening, Lizzy?" Jane asked with concern.

"I am … feeling unwell again," Elizabeth said. "We are only a … few houses away from Mr. Hurst's townhouse. I shall walk back there … to use their room. Can you ask John to come back for me …at the servant's entrance … after he takes you back to Gracechurch Street?"

"I shall walk back with you," Jane offered.

Elizabeth shook her head. "You are still as pale as a ghost, and Miss Bingley has a house full of sick patients. We had better not burden them again. I shall simply speak with the butler and he will admit me quietly. But it will be too cold for you and the horse to wait for me here. Travel on and then send the carriage back for me. It is the best solution for…everyone."

Jane agreed reluctantly, although she insisted that the carriage wait until she saw Elizabeth gain entrance to the Hurst residence. Then she travelled on.

When the door opened, Elizabeth told the butler that she had left a glove in the sitting room and asked him to locate it. Once the man had escorted her to a small side room to wait, she waited a few moments and then stepped cautiously out into the corridor again. Closing her eyes, she concentrated on Mr. Darcy.

As if she were viewing the entire plan of the house, she instinctively knew where to go. Quietly, with purpose, and without encountering a single servant, she reached the bedchambers on the upper floor.

How could that happened? Perhaps people could not see her when she was on angelic duty… But she had no time to waste on speculation about her possible discovery. Pushing the door open slowly and quietly, she saw Mr. Darcy lying on a bed. His eyes were closed, his lips moving as he murmured. His coat and waistcoat were gone.

Elizabeth locked the door and ran to his sides, shaking his shoulders to rouse him. "Mr. Darcy? Mr. Darcy, are you well?"

He half opened his eyes and said, "So sleepy…"

"We must leave." She patted his cheek. "Oh, do wake up! I fear Miss Bingley may have bad intentions towards you."

He continued to draw in shallow breaths but he did not move at all. Suddenly, Elizabeth heard the sound of voices outside the room. In a panic, she hurried to the door and grasped the handle, hoping to prevent whoever was out there from entering.

CHAPTER SEVEN

"Louisa is in her room," Elizabeth heard Miss Bingley say, her voice growing more audible as her footsteps neared the room. "She is sleeping."

"And Charles?" That was Mr. Hurst.

"In his room, as well," she replied. "Now, if you will excuse me, I have matters that require my attention."

"Both of them retiring in the middle of the day? Strange!" he said, pausing right outside the door. Elizabeth tensed. "And why are you here in the guest wing? I was not aware that we had any guests."

"I plan to check on some furnishings," she said.

"Shall I help you?"

"No, no, it is nothing," she said. "And I must take care of another matter before I begin." The sound of her footsteps faded down the corridor.

Nevertheless, the door handle beneath Elizabeth's hand vibrated slightly. Presumably, Mr. Hurst was preparing to check the room. But Elizabeth firmed her grip, holding it tight on the other side, and his strength proved to be no match for hers.

"Strange!" he murmured, abandoning the effort, and left.

Elizabeth finally dared to breathe again. Quietly, she released her hold on the handle and tiptoed back to look down at her ward. Hands on hips, she debated what she should do. A quick survey of the room revealed a painted china pitcher on a small table by the window. Fetching it, she leaned forward to splash drops of water onto his face, and was rewarded when he winced and groaned.

"Cold..." he protested and rolled suddenly towards her, flailing his arms in protest.

The uncoordinated gesture knocked the pitcher from her hand, sending water in all directions. Looking down, she saw with widened eyes that both her clothing and Mr. Darcy's had been drenched by the water.

As that unpropitious moment, he finally came awake.

"Elizabe – Miss Bennet! What are you doing?"

He sat up on the bed just as Elizabeth bent to retrieve the pitcher. Irresistibly, his gaze followed her movements, focusing on the gorgeous cleavage on display and her alluring form outlined by the clinging of her wet dress. Swallowing hard, he belatedly diverted his gaze, and asked in amazement, "Why are we in a bedroom?"

She retreated, clutching the water pitcher with one hand while she attempted to shield her chest from his scorching gaze, wondering how best to explain the incident and their present predicament to him. "It seems that you, Mrs. Hurst, Mr. Bingley and your sister were all overcome by sleep after drinking Miss Bingley's tea," she said at last.

He looked alarmed. "And you?"

"My sister and I both fell ill, but I am fine now. I do think, however, that you had better check on your sister's well-being."

When he nodded in agreement and rose, groaning, from the bed, Elizabeth's breath became shallow at the sight of his wet shirt-front and trousers.

They gazed at each other with an intensity potent enough to torch the room.

Click! Click!

The handle of the door lowered and the latch turned. Someone was about to discover them!

Elizabeth scanned the room in alarm. The armoire? No, that would be the most obvious place for anyone intent upon a search. Desperate, she looked at the bed and then, dashing past Mr. Darcy, dove under it.

A second later, to her astonishment, his hot body crowded in alongside hers. His eyes looked uncharacteristically bright in the darkness beneath the bed, and his lips were disconcertingly close, almost touching her face.

Merciful heaven, what possessed him to hide under the bed with me?

"What are you doing?" Elizabeth demanded, mouthing the words at him on the merest feather of breath.

He opened his mouth and replied, just as quietly, his lips grazing her earlobe, "Avoiding Miss Bingley."

She rolled her eyes and took a deep breath, which only served to envelop her in his musky scent.

Together, they listened to the slithering sound of fabric brushing the floorboards.

"Devil take him, where *is* the man?" That was definitely Miss Bingley, sounding waspish and exasperated. She paced over to the armoire, yanking it open and then slamming it shut again.

With a sigh that was nearly a growl, she stalked back to the bed. Elizabeth and Darcy held their breath as they felt the bed press against the tops of their heads.

Miss Bingley had actually sat down upon them!

"Damn that stupid Hurst!" she hissed. "He has spoiled my plan. Now Mr. Darcy is gone, when all I needed was the chance to lie down with him and wait for him to awaken. Just that simply, the position of the Mistress of Pemberley could have been mine!"

Under the bed, Darcy stiffened with outrage. Clearly, he would need to sever all connections with the woman forthwith.

Over their heads, they heard her laugh wickedly. "When my chance comes, I shall do more than just lie with him. I must see for myself how impressive he may be. Of course, Mr. Darcy has nearly the whole of Derbyshire to look after. Just as well! Then there will be no obstacles to prevent me from finding some fun on the side, after we marry."

Mr. Darcy took in more deep breaths, and Elizabeth saw his eyes narrow. She had never heard such a vulgar and mercenary commentary before. Even her mother, who was famous for her determination to find rich husbands for her daughters, was far less crude. *Poor Mr. Darcy! I wonder how many other scheming women have been sizing him up in such a way...*

Suddenly, Miss Bingley uttered a sound of startled disgust. "Water? Who woke him with water? If I find out...." For a moment, her angry breathing was the only sound in the room. "Ah well," she said at last, "he must still come back to collect his troublesome little sister. I shall have another chance then." With that, Miss Bingley rose and walked out of the room, closing the door behind herself with a petulant bang.

In her wake, the silence in the room was eerie. After a long moment, Mr. Darcy and Elizabeth dared to believe that Miss Bingley was truly gone. He wriggled out from under the bed first, then reached down to help Elizabeth out. When she had regained her feet, he bowed and said, "Miss Bennet, thank you for saving me from that horrible woman. And now I must see to my sister and see her safely home."

Elizabeth nodded. "Of course. Take care."

"And you? Is your coach ready? Where is Miss Jane?"

"You need not worry. I have made arrangements for my departure. Miss Bingley will not notice. Go to your sister with a clean conscience."

"Thank you." He took one last, lingering look at her lovely form before bowing again and leaving the room.

Once he was gone, Elizabeth laid claim to a bureau shawl and wrapped it around her neck, draping it to disguise the wet front of the dress and pinning it in place. Then she chanted, *"Crosswind and Whirlwind, I trust Ventara the God of Wind"*. With her wings spread, she opened the window and looked down at the inner courtyard, where several servants were currently occupied.

Taking a deep breath, she concentrated on the ground one floor below and flew down. She felt free, uplifted, especially since the servants seemed oblivious to her. For the first time, she felt truly happy to be an angel.

After she had landed, she went to a window through which she could observe the entrance. It was not long before she saw Mr. Darcy take his leave from Mr. Hurst hurriedly, with Georgiana bundled, fast asleep, in his arms. Once he had safely boarded his carriage, Elizabeth walked to the servant's entrance to wait, watching the servants go about their work for more than half an hour before she finally saw her uncle's coach arriving. As she went out of the door, she recited, *"Artful and Ample, I am just a normal angel."* At that, her wings were gone and her uncle's coachman was able to notice her presence, where he waited for her to board the carriage.

***

Miss Bingley, watching them from another room upstairs, chewed her lip and frowning. *Where did Miss Eliza come from? She was supposed to be gone! Did she spoil my plan? How did Mr. Darcy and his sister leave without notice? I must do something or he will be lost to me forever! And I shall consult that herbal doctor again.*

***

After Darcy had settled his sister, he retreated to the study and thought about the woman who created such havoc in his orderly life. The morning after the Netherfield Ball, he had awakened with a severe headache and the traces of having had sex again. After dining from a tray in his room, he tried to piece together the events of the previous evening: his dance and the argument with Elizabeth, then nursing his anger in the library with half a bottle of whisky, followed by rescuing her from Wickham.

Then things got crazy. He remembered growing very sleepy…and then, he could sworn, she had hurled him up and flown him to his bedchamber, where he clearly remembered experiencing the ecstasy of his life.

He remembered rubbing against her from behind, inhaling that delectable fresh-feather smell as he grazed his face on her soft wings.

And what about her own wild ride? The shaking of her lush twin peaks, the intensity of the passion displayed on her face, and the incredible profile of her wings, imprinted distinctly in his alcohol-dulled mind.

How could that be? Was he hallucinating? Being intimate with an angel? That would be more in Bingley's line. Shaken, Darcy had decided to leave the source of temptation and chaos behind. Pleading urgent matters to attend, he had fled to London, only to be surprised when the entire party from Netherfield packed up and followed him there.

But the increase in distance from Elizabeth had not decreased the longing in his mind. He found himself comparing every woman he met in town with her. None of them, however, was as witty, teasing and handsome as she. He would scowl at their figures and remember the feel of her gorgeous form...

After the New Year, his thoughts had become almost obsessive, as if he somehow knew that she was very near, almost within reach.

Sometimes, in a room full of people, he would find someone who looked a tiny bit like her from afar, and the most shocking thoughts would rush into his mind. He found himself thinking of how he would love to fondle Elizabeth's thigh, inside his box at the theatre when the curtain was raised and darkness surrounded them.

Or, when he was accompanying his sister to visit the modiste, he would look at some soft, exotic fabric and then have thoughts about tearing it, layer by layer, from Elizabeth's body, to reveal her alluring curves for his private enjoyment.

The most disturbing incident had been occasioned by seeing a woman on horseback, riding in the park. His mind flew off, creating images of riding naked with Elizabeth facing him, impaled upon him as they galloped like the wind.

These incidents left him frustrated and annoyed. Indeed, he often needed to be excused from the party he was with, to take time to calm himself.

Not one single night could he find sleep until he had fantasised about making love with her. In his thoughts, he would suckle her creamy mounds, lick her wet folds and stretch her hot inner muscles while he took himself to satisfaction.

Not that these fantasies brought him much relief. He would awaken the next morning feeling exhausted, hot, sweaty and deucedly unfulfilled.

He had almost decided to talk to Bingley about revisiting Hertfordshire, so that he could start a campaign to overcome his deep-seated dislike of her family, their lack of connections or wealth, so that he could formally begin to court her.

Instead, most unexpectedly, he had found her visiting Miss Bingley. In the minutes that followed, he grabbed every opportunity to prolong the visit, even insisting upon seeing the Bennet sisters back to their uncle in Cheapside so that he might invite them for dinner at his house.

But his plans had been thwarted. Looking back, he was furious with Bingley's sister. How dare she use a sleeping potion on them all? And Lord knew what wicked purgative she had inflicted on the Bennet sisters. Miss Bingley had deteriorated into a manipulative woman who had no scruples that were dearer to her than achieving her personal goal, by whatever evil means required. Anything seemed to be justifiable, in her twisted mind, so long as it enabled her to accomplish her aim of becoming Mistress of Pemberley.

And Elizabeth had come to his rescue yet again! Perhaps she *was* his guardian angel. She certainly reminded him of the brave little girl who, with Herculean strength, had managed to lift up the carriage in order to save his leg.

Darcy took another mouthful of the whisky and resolved to visit the Bennet sisters at Gracechurch Street, the next day, with or without Bingley.

***

The next morning, Bingley came to visit him, very early.

"Darcy, I do not understand what happened yesterday. We were chatting one minute and, the next, I awoke to find that it was supper time. I did not see to my guests. I was not even aware when you took your leave. I have come, this morning, to apologise."

"Did Hurst not tell you?"

"Hurst? He was his usual drunken self last night. He said nothing about the matter."

"Well, he helped me find Georgiana and led me out of the townhouse without encountering anyone. I thought he knew. I am afraid it was your sister's doing."

"Caroline? What are you saying? What did she do?"

"Miss Elizabeth told me that your sister used a sleeping potion on all of us."

Bingley stared at him in astonishment. "Surely that cannot be true! What would Caroline have hoped to achieve? And how did Miss Elizabeth discover it? What about her sister and herself?"

"Miss Bingley did not use a sleeping potion on them, but rather some herb designed to make them sick. Miss Elizabeth came back to find us, out of concern for our well-being, and happened upon me. I am sorry to have to tell you, I heard the most vulgar revelations from your sister with my own ears. I am sorry to pain you, Charles. But your sister intended to lie with me while I was drugged into sleep in order to compromise me and force me to offer for her."

Mr. Bingley dropped down heavily on the nearest chair, too shocked to stand.

Mr. Darcy continued in tones of iron decision. "I fear I shall have to cut all my connections with her, from this moment onward. Georgiana will not receive her any more, nor shall either of us visit you at the Hursts' abode."

Bingley nodded, holding his head in his hands. "I was utterly shocked to learn that she lied to Miss Bennet about our reasons for departing Hertfordshire. When you left Netherfield, the day after the Ball, she used a trumped-up excuse to make me follow you. She claimed to have forgotten some important jewels in town, and begged me most urgently to come and recover them for her. Then, before I could return, she closed the house, followed after us, and persuaded Louisa and Hurst to stay here for the winter as well.

"I see now that I was her unwitting dupe. She promised me that she had written to Miss Bennet to explain our absence, but soon she told me that Miss Bennet was so busy entertaining her cousin, the one who would one day become Master of Longbourn, that she had not even asked after me. I have been miserable ever since. Damn! I shall have to speak to Hurst and Louisa about it, and find some solution to curb her action. Perhaps we should send her to stay with our relatives in Ireland. But what about Miss Bennet? Is there any hope that she might still be willing to see me, after all of these dire strategies on my own sister's part?"

"Who can say? I, for one, plan to visit the Bennet sisters now, without delay. Come with me, and we will learn to our own satisfaction whether Miss Bennet is willing to meet you," Darcy said firmly.

To his relief, Bingley jumped up immediately and followed him willingly out of the door.

***

Elizabeth sat quietly in the drawing room, listening as Jane conversed with their cousins. The night before, after returning from her angelic duty, Elizabeth had immediately summoned Mihaela. From their discourse, she learned the truth of what she had come to suspect – that other people were unable to see the vision or hear the voice of an angel, excepting those whom the angel expressly intended to have see or hear.

When she was first learning to fly, in her bedchamber in Longbourn, her family had come to check on her not because they had heard her conversing with Mihaela, but because she was too clumsy and made such a thunderous noise on the floor when she dropped.

Now that Elizabeth knew Miss Bingley might cause Mr. Darcy harm, she asked the Lost Angel Commissioner to teach her other angelic skills, the better to protect him. She learned the new skills with eager interest but was unsure how she could carry out her duties if he remained in London while she was compelled to go on a visit to Kent. Mihaela told her she did not know, but that things always had a way of working out.

Elizabeth found it a singularly unsatisfactory response.

Now, as she sat lost in thought, contemplating how to find an excuse to prolong her stay in London, Mr. Darcy and Mr. Bingley were announced and shown into the room. The amiable gentleman moved to sit besides his lovely angel, Jane and her little cousins. Mr. Bingley immediately engaged in conversation with her, while the taller man and Elizabeth remained silent, sitting opposite each other.

Mrs. Gardiner came in and introduction was made. She used her considerable skill to draw the quiet pair into small talk, but the atmosphere in the room was rather strained. Thomas Gardiner, all of five years old, thought it strange and jumped into the conversation.

"Sir, it's impolite to stare at girls," he stated.

"Tommy!" his mother chastised.

Mr. Darcy's face turned bright red, as did Elizabeth's.

"Well, that's what you said when I kept looking at Emma, next door." Thomas argued. "And he has been staring at Lizzy since he arrived."

Before Thomas's mother could reprimand him again, Mr. Darcy shifted on his chair and found his voice. "You are quite right, Master Thomas. I should not stare at Miss Elizabeth so, but I find that she reminds me of someone I once knew."

"Who would that be?" Mr. Bingley asked. "I never heard you mention that before."

Mr. Darcy glanced at Elizabeth again before replying, "Miss Elizabeth resembles the little girl who saved my life during that carriage accident, long ago. I did not make the association until we spoke about the incident yesterday."

"Oh yes, the pretty little girl with expressive eyes and dark, curly hair," Jane said, "Lizzy, were you there when the accident happened?"

Elizabeth bit her lips, blushed, hesitated for a moment, and then nodded. "Yes. It was I. But I fear that Mr. Darcy is being far too lenient. You see, I caused the accident."

"What?" Bingley exclaimed. "Darcy has never said much about how the accident happened. What makes you think that you caused it?"

"I was playing near the main road," she confessed. "I threw a stone, and one of Mr. Darcy's carriage horses was startled by it."

"Bad Lizzy!" the younger Gardiner children exclaimed.

"She did not do that intentionally," Mr. Darcy asserted, coming immediately to her defence. "And she worked very hard to free my leg from under the carriage. No one was seriously hurt. I still thank your cousin whole-heartedly for her part in the affair."

Upon this revelation, the adults in the room looked at Mr. Darcy and Elizabeth with newly keen interest, as if their prior awkwardness and blushing had taken on new meaning. The conversation flowed much more easily, thereafter, and by the time the guests took their leave, Mr. Darcy had proposed a dinner invitation to the Gardiners. As the Mistress of the house, Mrs. Gardiner cheerfully accepted on behalf of her husband and her nieces, and it was clear, that everyone was eager to see what further intentions the tall gentleman might have towards his rescuer.

CHAPTER EIGHT

Mr. Darcy sat in the carriage and, as often as he dared, glanced at the lovely Miss Elizabeth sitting across him. Young Thomas Gardiner was sitting on his right, so he did not focus his gaze upon the object of his desire for long at any one time, in case the young boy might feel moved to renew his innocent remarks.

While Elizabeth chatted amiably with her aunt, who sat on her right, Darcy contemplated the evening ahead. He had asked Georgiana to place Elizabeth next to him during dinner. He hoped to have some entertaining conversation, even if other sorts of stimulation was precluded in such a public setting, and he hoped that he might even find an opportunity to probe her, discreetly, for more information about his dreams.

The other guests were riding with Mr. Bingley in his carriage, which had gone ahead a few minutes earlier.

But Darcy's musings were abruptly interrupted by a loud yell and a sudden jolting of the carriage. After several plunging lurches to the left and right, the carriage stopped altogether.

When he looked out of the window, he saw that they had stopped on a narrow lane.

"Are you all well, Mrs. Gardiner, Miss Bennet, Master Thomas?" he asked, and they all nodded, although still clearly a bit shaken by the incident.

He rapped on the ceiling of the carriage and called out, "Winton, what happened?"

"Someone threw a snake at us, sir," Winton replied, sounding somewhat breathless. "We've shaken it off now. Sorry about stopping so suddenly."

"No one is hurt. That is most important. Where are we now?"

"We turned from Annon Street and are near Salter's Hall on St. Swithins Lane."

Suddenly, Mr. Darcy saw four men with their faces covered rush out from the dark entrance of the Salter's Hall. In a matter of moments, they overcame both Winton and the driver.

Alarmed, Mr. Darcy reached to arm himself, but before he could remove the pistol from its secret compartment, one of the assailants pulled the carriage door open. A tall man with short coarse hair waved a knife and demanded, "All out, 'cept you, gentleman!"

Mrs. Gardiner drew in a shaky breath, took her frightened son's hand, and stepped out immediately. Elizabeth began to rise as well, giving Mr. Darcy an anxious look. Before she could get out of the carriage, however, another man clambered in. Pushing her aside, he sat down on the cushion that Mrs. Gardiner just vacated and hauled the door shut with a loud bang. Then the carriage lunged and began to move at speed. The man with the knife, caught off-guard by the sudden motion, tumbled to the carriage floor.

Elizabeth, losing her balance, dropped into Darcy's lap, and he wrapped his arm around her waist protectively from behind.

"Are you daft? There's still a woman in 'ere," the man on the floor protested, scowled up at his partner, who was short and bald.

"Somebody was coming," the bald man said, clearly unrepentant. "We'll drop her out of town."

Mr. Darcy tightened his hold, forcing a gasp from Elizabeth's lips, and said, "She is my fiancée," he said firmly, which elicited a second, very different gasp from Elizabeth. "If you abandon her out of town and she is harmed in any way, I shall not pay your ransom."

"Who said we want a ransom?" the bald man sneered, then added thoughtfully, "Though you do look quite rich..."

"What did you mean by kidnapping me, then, if not for ransom?"

"Shut up or I may just decide to enjoy your woman." He leaned forward and tried to grab Elizabeth by the jaw. She avoided his hand and buried her face against Mr. Darcy's chest. He enfolded her even more tightly and shifted to the side, the better to avoid the highwayman's hand.

"Stop it, Craze!" The tall kidnapper scrambled up and settled beside his partner. "She said there was to be no hurtin' him."

The bald man nodded reluctantly and leaned back, commenting on how comfortable the carriage was, then moving on to other unimportant topics, while Mr. Darcy and Elizabeth embraced each other, tense with concern about what might happen next.

They remained silent throughout the journey that ensued. Although it was comforting to hold Elizabeth close, breathing in her sweet lavender scent, feeling her soft form nestled on his lap, Mr. Darcy was deeply concerned about her safety, and he observed the passing scenes keenly. He could see that they were travelling south, and he wondered how long it would take his men to raise the alarm and organise a party to trail them.

Not long after they reached the outskirts of London, the kidnappers turned the carriage into a wooded area. Darcy tensed when it came to a halt in the middle of nowhere.

"Out you go," Craze said, and he and his partner flashed their knives. Darcy dared not put Elizabeth down in the carriage with the two men while he stepped out first, so he whispered to her, "I shall carry you out. Hold tight."

She nodded and wrapped her arms around his neck. When they stepped out of the carriage, they could see that another small coach was tied to a tree, not far away.

"What d'you say, guvner? Shall we leave your fiancée here?" Craze taunted, approaching them.

Another of the kidnappers said, "Quick. We don't want people chasin' after us, do we? Take 'em together. He have a tougher time trying' to run off with her along."

The other kidnappers agreed, despite Craze's scowl. After Mr. Darcy and Elizabeth boarded the small carriage, one of the four men climbed up to drive the horses, and Craze joined him on the box. The tall man chose to sit across from the captives. As soon as he was inside, the coach pulled out, leaving the fourth man behind – to deal with Darcy's carriage, or so he supposed.

"Where are you taking us?" he asked of the tall man, judging him to be less menacing than Craze had been.

The man shrugged and did not reply.

"Excuse me," Elizabeth said suddenly, "but who is this 'she' who said that you were not to hurt Mr. Darcy?"

"Th' rich lady."

Mr. Darcy and Elizabeth looked at each other. Unless their abductor thought all upper-class women to be rich, his statement would seem to rule out Miss Bingley, who was dependent on her family for her dresses and spending money.

"Did you meet her in London?" she asked, daring to probe him again.

He shook his head. "No, you'll not catch me livin' in town."

"Well, I hope you are not taking us across the Channel," she said companionably, "for I do not like the Frenchies."

"Bah! Frenchies has best drink. But we cain't go near 'em. Ain't like blood."

Elizabeth looked out of the carriage window. "It is getting colder and darker. Will we be travelling through the night to reach the rich lady?"

The kidnapper shook his head. "Too far for one night. We'll stop 'n sleep. Head arranged it."

"Has Head arranged for some dinner, as well? I am quite hungry now, and I am certain that you must be, as well."

The man made a sour face. "No more questions. I'm tired. We wait'd two days for your man." That said, he closed his eyes and settled into the corner of the carriage seat as if to sleep.

Darcy bent his face to hers and whispered, "I am sorry to have involved you in this unpleasant situation."

Despite the growing darkness, she could read the warmth and sincerity in his eyes. She shook her head and whispered back, "Do not distress yourself. Perhaps I am destined to be here."

"Whatever befalls us, I shall do my utmost to protect you." he vowed.

Thinking back over the several times when she had protected him when he was either drunk or half asleep, she could not resist smiling broadly. She raised her eye brows and replied archly, "I am quite capable of taking care of myself. Do you not remember me hitting Mr. Wickham in the woods?"

Reminded of what happened after that, Mr. Darcy gathered his courage and said, "I had the strangest…dream, after that incident." He drew a deep breath and continued, his eyes never leaving her face. "I dreamed that you had…wings. You flew me back to my bedchamber and we…" He leaned closer to her ear. "…and we …"

Heart racing, Elizabeth remembered that night vividly, as well. She said, "You were somewhat the worse for drink." Moving slightly back from him, she turned her head to look at him. "I left to find a servant..."

She realised that it was a mistake to have turned to look at him, as his face was still turned towards her, his mouth so very close....

Mr. Darcy felt as if he were drowning in her sweet scent. Her alluring cherry lips were within such easy reach that he nearly forgot about their predicament altogether. But before he could act on his desire, the coach slowed to a stop. Darcy moved to wrap his arms around Elizabeth's shoulder protectively once again. Looking out of the window, he could just discern the rough and neglected shape of a peasant cottage.

The tall kidnapper woke with a start as the door of the coach was pulled open.

"Out you get, Mister and your woman," Craze demanded, "It's cold and I'm tired."

Mr. Darcy stepped out as instructed and helped Elizabeth down, all the while aware of Craze hovering near them, as threatening as a thundercloud.

"The blanket on the floor at the end of the cottage is your bed," Craze said, flashing his knife. "The window's blocked and we be stayin' near the door. Dinna even think 'bout slippin' aways in the night, for it's your woman who'll suffer when I catch you."

Mr. Darcy and Elizabeth walked behind a damaged fence and entered the cottage, where they found a meager blanket spread. With a sigh, they sank down onto it.

"It is cold," Mr. Darcy whispered.

"At least we are in a sort of room, however rough," Elizabeth replied in a low voice. "I do not want Craze looking at us when we sleep."

He nodded his agreement. "I shall ask them for something to eat. You must be famished."

"Do not trouble yourself. They will give us something if they wish to. Otherwise, we had best not talk to them when Craze is about. We do not want to antagonise him, for he appears to fit his name all too well."

After a time, the tall kidnapper came to offer them some bread and water. When they had shared the scant meal, they retired to the blanket.

Remembering the near kiss in the coach, the two sat silent, feeling awkward with each other. At length, Elizabeth arranged her cloak to cover her body as fully as it could, and settled herself close to the wall, while Mr. Darcy used his greatcoat as a blanket.

He soon sensed that she was shivering. Moved towards her, he said, "It is a cold night, and your evening dress is made of thin muslin. Take my greatcoat, as it will do a better job of warming you."

She turned to look at him. Given all that she had allowed him to do while she was on angelic duty, she thought it silly of her to be missish now, and so, instead of depriving him of his greatcoat, she moved closer to him and slipped beneath it. Wrapping her arm around his waist, she rested her head on his chest. "Thank you."

Frozen by her embrace, he drew in a troubled breath that did nothing to ease the tightness in his chest. His heart began pounding loudly against his ribs, for he could feel her soft form moving against his hard body each time she took a breath. He soon found that it invoked a most pleasant memory in his mind, leaving him certain that they had lain together before.

If that were so, he reasoned, then perhaps everything that he recalled – the waltz, the library, the bedchamber – was true. *Is she really my guardian angel? Is that why she was confident that she could take care of herself? Have I fallen in love with an angel?*

He lowered his head and kissed her hair, while his hands wandered instinctively over her back. He could feel her lush bosom against his waistcoat. He wished with all his heart that they were somewhere else... Determined to calm himself, he thought about the kidnappers and their mastermind. Who would want to capture him? And for ＼ ２t, if it was not a question of ransom?

But his weary mind produced no answers, and finally he managed to drift to sleep.

***

Early the next morning, Mr. Darcy and Elizabeth were awakened by the bandits and were chivvied quickly back into the coach. Soon, torrents of rain began to fall as they made their way down one muddy lane after another. Mr. Darcy held onto Elizabeth throughout the journey, as Craze and the tall guy both insisted upon sitting opposite them, out of the weather.

By now, it was apparent to Mr. Darcy that they were moving towards Kent. The kidnappers were in such a hurry that they would not hear of stopping for food. The only breaks in the journey were short pauses to allow the horses to rest, from time to time.

As the carriage lumbered on towards its destination, Darcy's heart sank as he suspected increasingly that they were heading towards Rosings Park, the residence of his aunt, Lady Catherine de Bourgh. While she was certainly strong-willed enough to have organised his kidnapping, whyever would she do so? He was already scheduled to be there in a few weeks time. Why the hurry…?

With a pang, he remembered receiving several letters from his aunt over the past few days, letters which he had not yet opened. What had he done with them? He was never that negligent in his correspondence, but since his return from Hertfordshire to town, his mind was constantly distracted and his sleep disturbed.

Finally, very late on the second day of their ordeal, the carriage stopped, as he had foreseen, outside the church at Rosings Park. As soon as Mr. Darcy and Elizabeth had been forcibly escorted inside, the kidnappers shut the door of the church and departed.

"Finally!" An elderly woman, luxuriantly dressed, rose from her seat, waved her walking stick and demanded, in loud, angry tones, "Where have you been, my nephew? I have sent you two letters and an express within the past week."

"Aunt." Mr. Darcy bowed and replied, "I am most sorry for not replying sooner. I was …otherwise engaged, in town." He raised his chin and fixed her with a glare. "But how could you resort to taking me by force? Is there some dire emergency? Has something happened to Anne?"

"Force? Oh, do not be fanciful," Lady Catherine said with a dismissive sniff. "I only instructed Head to bring you here immediately. It is no kidnapping. As to an emergency, that is not the precise term that I would have chosen, but it is a matter of importance and it does indeed concern Anne. In fact, she and I have been waiting for you. It is high time that you and she married, and so I have arranged it, and have instructed Mr. Collins to perform the ceremony."

Mr. Darcy was astonished. He perceived, for the first time, that the clergyman was indeed standing off to one side, obsequious and silent. And nearby, slumped in one of the pews was his cousin, Anne, dressed in bridal finery. She appeared to be half-conscious, and Maria Lucas, the young girl who was a good friend to Elizabeth's younger sisters, was supporting her.

Alarmed, he walked quickly to Anne's side. She was unconscious but breathing. When he touched her forehead, he found that she was burning hot.

"Aunt," he said angrily, "I have no desire to marry Anne, as you well know. And she is not fit for any ceremony, at the moment. Clearly, she is ill. We must take her back to the house and summon the doctor immediately."

"No desire to marry Anne?" Lady Catherine seemed to swell before their eyes, a portrait of fury. She moved near to Mr. Darcy and thumped her walking stick on the ground several times. "The match was agreed by your sainted mother. It was her dearest wish. You and Anne have been destined for each other since the cradle. Anne contracted a fever, a week ago, and has not been improving. That is why I sent for you to come earlier. But she will be fine, once she is married to you. Mr. Collins, commence with the ceremony."

Mr. Darcy stared at her. "You must be mad." He stood up and turned to Mr. Collins, "You, there. Come and carry my cousin back to the house." Mr. Collins paled and looked at his patroness, clearly undecided. "Immediately!" Mr. Darcy commanded. The clergyman finally came forward and, with difficulty, picked up the sickly young woman. "Return her to her chambers and send a servant to fetch the doctor to attend to her immediately." he added.

"Not so hasty!" Lady Catherine yelled. "Unhand my daughter, Mr. Collins! Head, Craze, bring my nephew to the altar. This wedding will begin immediately."

The bandits, who clearly had been awaiting her summons, came back via another entrance on their Ladyship's command. The three men advanced towards Mr. Darcy but he avoided them, moving around the pews as he continued to argue with Lady Catherine.

"Aunt, have you taken leave of your senses? I cannot possibly marry Anne, not least because your kidnapping scheme forced Miss Bennet and myself to spend last night together. I must marry *her* now, since I have compromised her."

When Darcy attempted to rush to Elizabeth's side, the three men blocked his way.

His words made the grand lady aware of the young woman inside the church for the first time. Lady Catherine turned to look at Elizabeth's disheveled appearance and raised scandalised brows. "Miss Bennet? That cousin of Mr. Collins's? Do be serious, Darcy. She has an uncle in trade and no dowry at all. Mr. Collins tells me that her mother and younger sisters are the silliest sort of geese, with no sense of propriety. For your sake, I shall give her a hundred pounds. She can satisfy herself with that and be gone, leaving you free to marry Anne as you ought."

Outraged by Lady Catherine's remarks, Elizabeth folded her arms, burning to retort, but Mr. Darcy beat her to it despite the fact that he was struggling with the three men now.

"I know perfectly well that she has no connection and no dowry, and that some of her family display a total lack of propriety. But I have been in love with her since nearly the first moment that I met her. Hear me, Aunt, and believe my words – I shall marry Miss Bennet, no matter what you say to the contrary."

Elizabeth could scarcely believe what she was hearing. *He loves me? How can that be? I thought he only lusted after me, a rake who trifled me when he was drunk. Nevertheless, how can he declare loving me one minute and degrading my family the next?*

For the moment, she resolved to leave Mr. Darcy and his aunt to fight amongst themselves. But before she had taken two steps towards the church door, she heard him cry out in pain.

Whirling back, she saw that knives had been introduced into the struggle, and someone had apparently stabbed him in the arm. The three men had nearly succeeded in wrestling him to the ground.

Her angelic instinct overwhelmed her. Without a second thought, she chanted her angelic verse and spread her wings. Then, using some of the newly acquired skills she had learned from Mihaela, she chanted, *"Cirrus and Cumulus, I trust Cephrus, the God of Cloud"*. With that, she swirled her index finger, stirring up a gust of wind that blew the villains away from her ward. With a curve of her palm, she summoned a thick cushion of cloud that lifted Mr. Darcy into the air. She blew the cloud steadily so that it bore him out of the church and carried him a short distance away.

Inside the church, the women screamed and the men gaped, their mouths wide open, totally stunned as they watched Mr. Darcy's departure on a cloud. Not one of them, however, witnessed the disappearance of Miss Bennet in her angelic form.

Taking note that the air was cold, and that her ward's arm was bleeding, she propelled him to a small cottage at the other end of the estate. By the time they had both landed safely on the ground, he was agog.

"We were flying!" He regarded her with widened eyes. "You *are* an angel!"

Without replying, she pushed opened the door of the cottage. The little building was old and simply furnished, but in good order. Lighting a candle, she placed a chair by the table. "Come and sit. Let me dress your wound."

Mr. Darcy sat obediently and let her attend to his injury, which proved not to be very serious. At any rate, he did not feel the pain. He was still in a daze from discovering her angelic identity.

Elizabeth tore a length of muslin from the hem of her dress and bound his cut. By the time she was finished, he had recovered his senses. Gently, he raised her chin and looked at her with sober intensity.

"Why did you allow the things that happened between us in the library and in my room at Netherfield?" he asked, the words seeming to burn in his throat. "Are you a fallen angel? Are you here to tempt me to forget my honour, my obligations and my duty to family and friends?"

CHAPTER NINE

Mr. Darcy removed his hand from her chin, then rose and began to pace. "I have been so blind. I had spent weeks and months debating with myself about whether I should offer for you, a woman with inferior connections, one whose family members exhibit a total lack of propriety. But now it appears that you are not even real! You almost tempted me to commit a carnal sin when I was exhausted and when I was under the influence of alcohol. What sort of person – no, spirit – has claimed my heart? And to what purpose?"

"Tempted you? You are most mistaken, Mr. Darcy." Deeply wounded, Elizabeth stood up and said angrily, "I would never agree to marry you, even if you were the richest man in the whole of England. Very soon after my re-acquaintance with you, I observed you to be arrogant and conceited, and to possess a distressingly selfish disdain of other people. And now your ungentlemanly thoughts reinforce my understanding of your character." Elizabeth was pacing now, as well. "Dare you claim that *I* tempted you to commit the carnal sin? I am an innocent, sir. You and your scandalised thoughts were to blame."

"How so?" Mr. Darcy approached her. "If memory serves me correctly, I never forced myself on you. You responded most passionately to my kisses."

"I am your guardian angel. I learned only recently that I had been accidentally dropped from Heaven and had therefore been unable to guard you for over twenty years. It was ruled that, because I had not previously performed my duties, I was required to cater to your wishes. I hate being your guardian angel! And I hated submitting to your licentious thoughts and advances!"

"Cater to my wishes? Nonsense!" He laughed roughly, then wrapped his arms around her waist, pulling her against his body. "Let us see how you 'hate' my licentious thoughts now. I will have you moaning in ecstasy soon!"

Lowering his head, he sucked her upper lip as if he intended to draw out the very essence from her body. Shivering violently, she struck his chest, determined not to have any more scandalous encounters with him. Gathering her strength, she pushed at him, struggling to get away.

He let go of her, in the end. But when she tried to fly out of the door, he sat down again on the chair, folded his arms and demanded, "Come back here, my angel!"

Her feet froze. Most unwillingly, she turned and walked slowly back to him. "I hate you!" she exclaimed.

When she was mere inches from him, he gazed at her with a wicked gleam in his eyes. "My word, what a sweet and appealing angel you are! I have been an honourable gentleman my entire life, with few forbidden thoughts or vile behaviours to my account until I met you, last year. Maybe this is the Lord's way of rewarding me – to present me with a personal angel, a love slave to command as I wish. Now, my beautiful Elizabeth, step out of your pretty slippers and remove your dress."

She stepped out of her shoes, trembling with anger, and said vehemently, "You will be punished for using me like this." Much to her disgust, she found herself compelled to chant the angelic verse that hid her wings. Then her hands, as if of their own volition, moved to her back and unfastened the buttons. Loosened, the evening gown dropped to the ground, pooling around her bare feet.

Mr. Darcy could not think straight. Elizabeth's wings were gone, and she really was doing as he bid. Panting, he whispered, "Continue." His gaze never left her, and he found himself wishing that the candle light within the cottage was brighter.

Biting her lower lip, she pushed down her chemise, stays and stockings. When she stood before him in full glory, she raised her chin and speaking distinctly, proclaimed, "I hate you!"

But he did not hear her at all. He was devouring her body with his gaze. Previously, when they were intimate, he had not been himself. This time, by contrast, he was determined to commit her every curve and response to memory. Even if she was right, and he would be punished for using his guardian angel in such a way, he could not repent of it, for now he could die a happy man, with the image of her in the forefront of his mind. He could not find the will to care about tomorrow. He simply wanted her, now!

"Come and straddle my lap."

She squared her jaw and walked to him. When he did not relent, she had no choice but to place her hands on his shoulders and take a seat on his thighs.

Mr. Darcy was trembling, each breath coming hard. The woman he had desired for so many months was sitting on him, gloriously naked. Her cherry lips were inches from his hungry mouth. Her ample bosom was almost brushing his chest, the rosy nipples tight-gathered in the cold air, begging to be nipped. And the lush bush of curls at her apex was positioned tantalisingly close to his arousal.

Suddenly, with the sweet lavender scent of her skin flooding his nostrils, he could no longer bear simply looking at her voluptuous body. Moving his hands around to encompass her buttocks, he drew her closer to him. Then, bending his neck, he nibbled her smooth shoulder and the delicate curve of her throat, feeling the pulse that beat there so frantically. He traced his lips and teeth along the upper swell of her bosom and then, with a groan of delight, took possession of her nipple. He suckled hard, like a desperate infant who had not been fed for days. One of his hands stole up to squeeze the other breast, and he plucked at her nipple, teasing the sensitised peak.

Elizabeth was unprepared for such wild ministrations. Overcome, she let her head loll and arched her back, offering up her bosom for him to feast upon, while her legs instinctively clasped his thighs enthusiastically.

Mr. Darcy gasped as her squirming nearly caused him to explode but he calmed himself and continued the exploration for endless minutes.

When he felt that she was ready for him, rising on wobbly legs, he turned and lowered her onto the table, without releasing her breast from his ardent kiss. With the utmost urgency, he opened his breeches, positioned himself with precision, and thrust himself slowly, against her hot, wet entrance.

"Oh!" Elizabeth cried out in pain as he broke through her barrier, but almost immediately she experienced an upwelling of incredible sensations rising from where he was now so intimately joined with her. Her hands grasped frantically at the edges of the little table, bracing her as she received his next forceful push, one which sank him right to the hilt.

There he stopped, suspending both his thrusting and his kiss for a frozen moment, savouring the ineffable sensation of being buried completely inside of her. For the first time, he felt utterly clear-headed about what he was doing. He could feel every inner wet muscles of her tight core, embracing and squeezing his hot, hard shaft. He saw her disheveled hair spread out on the table around her shoulders, her mouth open and panting, her eyes tight-closed, her creamy, pink-peaked mounds covered with his love bites.

He worshipped her. She was the handsomest woman of his acquaintance. He wanted to bring her to new heights, to have her gaze at him in adoration as she screamed with ecstasy.

Taking a deep breath, he raised her legs from his waist and draped them over his shoulders, elevating her core.

Elizabeth felt the change in every fibre of her being. He seemed to be touching her in places she had not even known existed within her, his massive presence awakening some new and desperate appetite in her very core. Shivering with anticipation, blushing at the exposed position, she opened her eyes and looked up at him with an unspoken question burning in her gaze. Her hands moved to grab his waist.

He replied by beginning to move again, withdrawing slightly, the better to establish a new rhythm, invading and retreating, thrusting in and out, creating a path of heated friction within her, slowly at first, then faster and faster. Soon, his frantic pounding shook her whole body, as well as the hard-used table. Her beasts swayed, agitated by the motion, treating him to an extreme of visual pleasure as he strove.

Pouring every dream and fantasy into his movements, he burrowed into her for what seemed an eternity, until her voice became hoarse from screaming out in pleasure. He finally tipped her past the borders of her control by grinding his tip into her core in a circular, hip-driven motion that ignited her senses and delivered her to a howling ecstasy of release. And still he labored on, thrusting into her a few, last, violent times before, with a roar, he reached his own all-encompassing peak and then collapsed on top of her, their bodies still deeply conjoined.

Slowly, he became aware that the cottage was cold. Mr. Darcy straightened and, reluctantly, withdrew his body from hers. Then he scooped Elizabeth up from the table and carried her to the little bed on the far side of the room. Even after he set her down, she was strangely silent, gazing up at the ceiling with half-opened eyes as he lit a fire, collected her clothes, and returned to snuggle next to her on the narrow pallet.

Faced with her moody countenance, he felt a sudden shame at his actions. *What claim can I make now to my good breeding and gentlemanly upbringing?* He wondered in belated contrition. *I as good as demanded her to act the part of my whore.* Brushing a wayward curl from her forehead, he kissed her cheek tenderly and said, "I am so sorry, Elizabeth. I do not know what came over me. Believe me when I tell you that I love you with all my heart."

She turned reluctantly to gaze at him, and a single silent tear dropped from her eye. "You cannot love me."

"But I do! You are witty, and intelligent, and the handsomest woman I have ever known." He kissed away the tear. "When a man loves a woman, he cannot help thinking of loving her physically all of the time. Will you forgive me for taking your virtue just now? Will you marry me?"

"I cannot marry you." She turned her face away, directing her gaze at the ceiling once again.

"Why? Because you are an angel?" He placed his finger on her chin and turned her face towards him again. "I thought you said that you had to cater to my wishes."

A shadow of anger flared in her eyes. "I shall return to Heaven one day. What do you suppose people will say if your wife suddenly disappears?"

Such a possibility had not occurred to him. He felt shocked, as if someone had punched him in the stomach. *It has taken me so many years to find the one I love. Why could she not have been a simple woman?* Forcing himself to breathe deeply and asked, "When will you have to go?"

"I do not know. The other angel who found me said that when the time came, I would know it undeniably."

"But that could be years away! We *must* marry. I have compromised you. I love you. If – when – you must leave me, I will bear with it as best I can." He lowered his head and kissed her frantically on the mouth.

Her lips did not soften beneath his caress. "But I do not love *you*. You are arrogant…" She was stopped mid-sentence by another kiss, and this time he felt her respond to his ardour.

Marginally heartened, he said, "What do you propose to do then? How else can we explain the situation to our family and friends except by matrimony?"

"I do not know. I shall think of something, later. Kiss me again. I do not want to think now."

He struggled against a sense of anger and hurt feelings. *She does not want to marry me! She says she does not love me. How could I have been so wrong? Shaken, he wished he had not declared his love to her so openly.*

As if Elizabeth were realising that she loved his attentions even if she did not love the man, and that this might be their last time ever to be together, she began smoothing her fingers across his chest, she started unbuttoning his clothes. When one of her hands lowered to the half buttoned up breeches which Mr. Darcy had done up after their previous love making, he was a lost man, forgetting about everything but the moment. He stripped off his clothes in seconds. Then, with a tender kiss on her lips, he began to woo her body with his own for the first time, skin to skin chest to chest, hip to hip and thigh to thigh. Her skin was smooth, like warm water, and she was soft where he was hard.

When his fingers took possession of her bounteous breasts, he felt her begin to caress his back, drawing circles with her fingertips. Her ministration made him shudder with need. All too soon, he felt the need to position himself over her apex, as he rubbed her moist folds with gentle insistence.

"Love me," she moaned.

"Say my name." He rubbed harder against her.

"Love me, Mr. Darcy," she whispered, gasping at the sensation.

He halted his ministrations. "No, call me Fitzwilliam."

"Do not stop, Fitzwilliam," she entreated, and slid her hands down his back to grasp his buttocks. "Come into me, please. I need you."

No further reassurance was required. He pushed into her slowly, intent on savouring every minute of mating with her. Inch by inch, he moved inside her, savoring the grip of her tight inner muscles, until he had buried himself to the hilt. She was his, forever and eternity. They had become one soul.

"Ride me," she invited huskily, her body impatient as it shifted beneath him.

He responded willingly, withdrawing almost to her entrance, then thrusting deeply into her in a slow glissade. But she wanted more. She arched her body to meet him, urgent and demanding. Like a wild creature, she seemed determined to shatter his control into pieces. And she soon succeeded, especially when her curious fingers traced downward from the base of his spine, exploring the shallow furrow below.

At her first intimate touch between his clenching buttocks, she felt him shiver. When, emboldened, her exploration grew more intrusive, it galvanised him wonderfully, and he began to pound into her like a mad man possessed. All the while, she was in ecstasy. Her mouth was filled with his strong lips and tongue. Her twin peaks were being forcefully shaped and squeezed, nipples puckered into hard pebbles of excitement. Her invaded womanhood was stretched to its limits, plundered by his huge, hard shaft, igniting a bonfire within her very core.

She needed him, needed this and needed it all to help her forget her duty and her imminent departure from this world and everything she knew. On and on, again and again, she moved with him, meeting him thrust for thrust until, abruptly, her body shivered and convulsed. Her soul flew out of her body, higher and higher, until every sense and feeling she possessed melted in ecstasy. She was in heaven again, with this handsome man who loved her to pieces and whom, despite her protestations, she loved with all her heart.

***

After they finally recovered from the exhausting efforts of their love-making, Mr. Darcy asked more questions about her angelic experiences, and she, in turn, questioned him about his aloofness towards the Meryton populace.

He explained to her how unhappy he had been when Wickham began trying to usurp his father's love, when Mr. Darcy had just turned eight. Then his mother died at Georgiana's birth. Although he loved his sister and Pemberley, he ever after felt alone and incomplete, isolated by his myriad responsibilities and duties.

He recounted to Elizabeth how Wickham had declined the living meant for him, choosing instead to exchange it for a handsome sum. He then explained how the scoundrel had squandered all of the money within a short few years, after which he had the effrontery to come back and demand the original living again. Failing in that effort, he had then schemed to elope with Georgiana, for the sake of her dowry and the revenge it would represent on Darcy himself.

Mr. Darcy also confided to her how much insincerity he discerned among strangers who attended him only because of his fortune and his position in society. But all of that had changed, after he crossed Elizabeth's path. He soon fell in love with her, and now he wanted nothing more than to spend the rest of his life with her. She and she alone made him feel complete.

Elizabeth sighed, heavy-hearted. "We should not marry, Fitzwilliam," she reiterated. "In fact, it would be best if we did not see each other again, after today. If we wed, we will only be miserable when the time comes when we must part forever." But his explanation concerning his wariness with strangers had touched her heart, changing her fundamental understanding of past events, and it made her inexpressibly sad to think of never seeing him ever again.

"I cannot agree," he said stoutly. "I do not care how long we will have, so long as we value the time that remains to us." He kissed her passionately again. "In fact, we should never part again, from this day onwards, since we cannot know how long together we may have."

Elizabeth, touched by this logic of the heart, returned his urgent ardency, and they made love yet again before finally drifting off to sleep in each other's arms.

***

At daybreak, Elizabeth woke first. Determined to save him from further misery, she found a scrap of paper and left him a note, then slipped out of the cottage and went in search of Mrs. Collins. After she had settled the matter of her departure with Maria, she tidied herself as best she could, completing her ablutions just as a coach drew up to the parsonage.

"Papa! Whyever are you here?" Elizabeth asked in astonishment upon seeing her parents descend from the coach.

"Lizzy! Oh, my Lizzy, you are safe!" Mrs. Bennet, rushing to her side, hugged her tightly and sobbed aloud. "I cannot *bear* it if you are taken away from me again."

Elizabeth was stunned. Her mother did not consider her the favourite and had seldom shown her much affection. She knew that her mother loved her, in her own peculiar way, but she was very touched by her expression of worry over her safety. Elizabeth hugged her back.

"Come, Fanny, we should go inside." Mr. Bennet said. Elizabeth was surprised at the tender tone of his voice.

"I do not see the reason for all this fuss and the rush," a new voice said, and Elizabeth turned to see Lydia jumping down from the coach. "Lizzy, did the highwaymen ravish you? Did you enjoy it? Were they handsome?"

At that, Mrs. Bennet gasped and swooned.

"Lydia!" both her father and sister chastised.

Seeing that her father was furious, Lydia shut her mouth and went inside to greet Maria instead.

Mrs. Collins showed the guests into the house and arranged to have Mrs. Bennet settled in a room. As Mrs. Bennet finally recovered from her nerves, after an application of smelling salts, she realised that her husband was holding her hand.

She turned to look at Elizabeth with teary eyes and asked, "Lizzy, has anyone hurt you?"

Elizabeth shook her head. "No, we were not precisely abducted. Mr. Darcy's aunt, Lady Catherine de Bourgh, wanted to see him urgently, as her daughter Anne is experiencing a high fever, and so Lady Catherine sent some servants to require

Mr. Darcy and his sister to come to Kent immediately. But they missed connecting with him at his house and followed him to Cheapside. Finding him there – and not unreasonably apprehensive about the delay, given the temper of their employer – they were somewhat overzealous and compelled his immediate departure by force. I was also in the carriage, most unfortunately, and they mistook me for Mr. Darcy's sister, Miss Georgiana Darcy. At any rate, when we changed carriages outside of London, Maria was waiting for us there."

Maria nodded enthusiastically to confirm this.

"They had brought her along to make sure that Miss Darcy was comfortable, so Maria was with me nearly the whole time. Lydia, I am sorry to disappoint you, but there was no highwayman. Yesterday, the rain was heavy and we did not arrive here till late. I was going to send you an express today but you came instead." Elizabeth continued.

"How can Her Ladyship have such stupid servants?" Mrs. Bennet said. "I feared the worst for you when I heard from your Uncle Edward that Mr. Darcy and you were kidnapped! And why were you in a carriage with that horrible man in the first place? Edward said Mr. Darcy seemed besotted with you, but I think my brother must be going mad. Mr. Darcy has never looked at any woman in Hertfordshire twice. And you hate him for slighting you."

Elizabeth's face turned a shade of pink as she replied, "Jane and I encountered him, along with Mr. Bingley, at Mr. Hurst's house. And I have found that he does improve upon closer acquaintance. He has been very nice to me, both in London and during this journey down to Kent. But how did you know to come here to find me?"

"Miss Darcy asked her cousin, Colonel Fitzwilliam, for help on the night that you two disappeared." Mr. Bennet said. "They traced the Darcy carriage to Maidstone and found one of the highwaymen – that is to say, one of Her Ladyship's servants, the next morning. The Colonel sent an express to relate that to Miss Darcy while he travelled from Maidstone to here directly. We left Longbourn for London on first light that day, as well, after we received Edward's express overnight. So when we heard the news yesterday morning in London, we also travelled here immediately. But the heavy rain slowed our progress horribly. I expected the Colonel would have arrived at his aunt's place late last night or this morning as well. So then, is Her Ladyship's daughter still unwell? And how is Mr. Darcy?" Mr. Bennet asked.

Right at this moment, the door bell rang. Together with Mr. Bennet, Elizabeth and Lydia, Mrs. Collins greeted Mr. Darcy and Colonel Fitzwilliam and performed the introduction.

Elizabeth's face turned bright red as her eyes glanced at Mr. Darcy. He looked serious, and she chewed her lip, hoping that he would go along with her story.

"Mr. Bennet, I am sorry that my aunt's actions involved Miss Elizabeth indirectly," Mr. Darcy apologised.

"Elizabeth explained the circumstances to us. How is your cousin, Miss de Bourgh?"

"She still has a high fever but a doctor is treating her now. My aunt is indisposed, as well, after last night's incident. Mr. Collins has been very … uhm… helpful. He remains at Rosings to assist," Colonel Fitzwilliam said.

"Yes, my cousin is most loyal to his patron," Mr. Bennet said.

"May I request a private meeting, Mr. Bennet?" inquired Mr. Darcy.

Elizabeth looked at him in alarm. She did not want the two men to speak privately, especially not before he had been enlightened as to her fabrications, and so she drew a deep breath and said, "If you are feeling concerned about possible repercussions from the actions of your aunt's servants, be assured that I have explained to my father that Mrs. Collins has been with me since we changed carriages outside of London, two nights ago."

Maria nodded her head emphatically again.

Darcy hesitated, determined not give up, but unwilling to flatly refute Elizabeth's story in front of the gathering.

Mr. Bennet saw the tension between the man and his daughter, and decided to get to the bottom of it. "Lizzy, I am sure Mr. Darcy just wants to assure me that nothing will befall you and Lydia during your stay here. Mrs. Collins, may Mr. Darcy and I use your husband's study?"

Clearly, there was no way to avoid such a civil request. "But of course," Maria said, and showed them the way.

Elizabeth wanted to stamp her foot in frustration. "Stubborn man!" she swore beneath her breath, and watched with foreboding as the two men vanished from her view.

CHAPTER TEN

"So then, what can I do for you, Mr. Darcy?" Mr. Bennet asked, once they settled inside the study.

Mr. Darcy paced around the room for a few second, then stood still to deliver his request. "Sir, I would like to ask your permission to marry your daughter, Miss Elizabeth."

Shocked, Mr. Bennet helped himself to a glass of wine. "How very interesting, since I do not recall your having asked my permission to court Elizabeth in the first place. How did this speedy courtship happen? When did she agree to marry you?"

Determined to mend his arrogant ways, Darcy concentrated on the most important thing at hand. "I have loved Miss Bennet since her stay at Netherfield. She is caring, witty and the handsomest woman I have ever known. It would be my greatest honour to call her my wife."

Although the man was exceptionally wealthy and handsome, Mr. Bennet would not part with his favourite without making certain that she would be happy. "That is all well and good but you have not answered yet my questions, young man."

Not wanting to lie, Darcy carried out his plan of action. "If you ask Miss Bennet to come in and join us, I suspect she would be more eloquent at explaining our courtship and her decision."

"You requested a private meeting. Are you not prepared to take up the responsibility of explanation?"

"Surrounded by a roomful of people, I could hardly request Miss Bennet to come with us for a private meeting."

Agreeing reluctantly, Mr. Bennet went to invite his daughter to join them.

When Elizabeth entered the room, Elizabeth gave Mr. Darcy a censorious glare. He returned it with an intense and yet somewhat self-satisfied expression.

The exchange was not lost on Mr. Bennet. "Lizzy," he said, "I have the most extraordinary news. Mr. Darcy has requested my permission to marry you. He says that he fell in love with you during your stay at Netherfield. However, as I recall, he left Hertfordshire immediately after the ball. Since you two met up again only days ago, in London, I do not see how the courtship could have proceeded. He has declined to give me an explanation, suggesting that you would be more eloquent in reply."

She gave Mr. Darcy another glare, debating how to advise her father to refuse the young man's offer. But before she opened her mouth, Mr. Darcy 'spoke' to her silently.

Remember, my angel, you must cater to my wishes or be guilty of dereliction of your duty. I do truly wish to marry you. I do not care how short-lived our time together may prove to be, so long as we make the most of this precious opportunity.

Frustrated by his stubbornness, she replied silently in anger. *But I do not wish to marry you. What joy would you find with a reluctant wife?*

Smiling, he said with confidence. *Being your husband would be an extraordinary source of happiness to me, both in and out of our bed. I cannot imagine, on the whole, that I would have any cause to repine.*

Insufferable man! Did you have to talk about our union in front of my father? Elizabeth's face turned bright red and her eyes flashed.

"Lizzy, are you well?" her father asked with concern. He had been turning his head back and forth, from Mr. Darcy to her, through their silent exchange, wondering whether they were engaged in some silent battle of wills.

"I am... well, Father," she said faintly.

Remember my wish! Mr. Darcy insisted.

Drawing a deep breath, she yielded. "I have been... attracted to Mr. Darcy since my stay at Netherfield. He left Hertfordshire to prepare his affairs."

"Am I to understand that the two of you reached an understanding after the short few days of your stay at Mr. Bingley's house?" Totally unprepared for such a confession, Mr. Bennet raised his voice in consternation. "But I distinctly recall that Jane received a letter from Miss Bingley, stating that they left because Mr. Darcy had been taken ill."

"I regret to inform you that Miss Bingley invented that story for mysterious reasons of her own." Mr. Darcy said.

Mr. Bennet turned back to face his daughter. "So you love this man and you wish to marry him? If he is attempting to force you in any way, take courage and tell me at once. I do not care if he is the richest man in the whole of England, I shall throw him out and prevent him from troubling you ever again."

Remember that you need to protect me, my angel. You do not want your father to harm me, or even think ill of me, Mr. Darcy told her.

Incorrigible man! I do not know what I have done in my past lives to deserve being assigned as your angel, she retorted.

And I believe, in turn, that I must have done much good in my past lives to deserve you, my dear, Mr. Darcy replied sweetly.

Elizabeth had the greatest urge to smack him and ignore his demands, but her hands, metaphorically, were bound. She nodded to her father and said, "Yes, Father, I do want to marry him. I love him."

As she uttered the words, she realised suddenly that they were true. After the kidnapping, she had gotten to know his feelings and character much better. The ups and downs of her dealings with him throughout their acquaintance had incited strong feelings in her, as well. His welfare and his person had gained importance in her mind, over the past few months. Despite the array of unsettling emotions he sometimes inspired, she believed that she wanted the best for him. She truly cared about him and wanted to take care of him.

Elizabeth closed her eyes and felt tears welling up. *How can I love him as a wife ought to when I cannot give him an heir? I am not even been allowed to stay with him for very long. Will I ever be able to forget him, when I am back in Himins? Will he ever be able to forget me? Why must my life be so complicated? Why can I not be an ordinary woman? I want to stay with him forever and bear his children.*

She suddenly felt extremely tired, as if her legs no longer had the strength to support her...

Before Darcy's and Mr. Bennet's horrified gaze, Elizabeth crumpled to the floor.

Both men rushed to her side, the younger reaching her first. He cradled her in his embrace and asked with concern, "My love, what is the matter? Are you ill?" He patted her face gently a few times but she did not wake up. Mr. Darcy swept her up into his arms and told Mr. Bennet, "I shall take her up to a bedchamber."

The older man opened his mouth, clearly wanting to protest, but Mr. Darcy strode past him. As Mr. Darcy passed the front room, he called peremptorily for Mrs. Collins to show him to a guest room, and demanded that his cousin summon the doctor from Rosings Park.

***

Lydia Bennet, observing the commotion, did not understand why the arrogant man was carrying her sister around. "Every one is sick in this house," she murmured. At a loss for how to occupy herself, she decided to go out and explore.

One lane led to a wooded area, another to the great house, and a third seemed to lead to the church.

"It is so boring here!" she complained aloud, and decided to leave the path and walk through the woods. After a quarter of an hour, however, she feared that she was lost. Upon hearing the approach of a horse, she was greatly relieved. She did not care overly for walking, and she was growing weary from wandering around. Eager for relief, she ran towards a clearing and saw, sitting atop a magnificent white horse, the handsome person of Mr. Wickham.

"La, fancy meeting you here, Mr. Wickham! We have missed you dearly in Hertfordshire." Lydia batted her eyes. She was happy she had decided to take off her Spencer a few moments earlier. As she bent to offer him a deep curtsey, she was certain that her bountiful bosom would show to its best advantage, since he was high on his horse.

Mr. Wickham smiled brightly, bowed as best as he could on horseback, and said, "I am extremely delighted to see you again, Miss Bennet. I have missed your lively conversation very much. Are all of your family members well?"

"Oh, Mother and Lizzy are sick. Mr. Darcy is looking after Lizzy. Such a bother. But let us not talk about them. Why did you leave Meryton so suddenly? Why are you here? I declare, my neck hurts, looking at you so far above me. Will you not dismount and sit with me for a while?"

"Of course." Mr. Wickham jumped down from the horse, removed his greatcoat and spread it on a fallen log.

Lydia made another curtsey before sitting down.

Another easy task, Wickham smiled. *I made the right decision to leave Hertfordshire. Not only did I hook up with Anne de Bourgh again, I shall get to sample the defying*

Lizzybell's younger sister. Lydia is a bit on the plump side, compared to her sister, but it will be grand to be able to boast, in the future, that I at least got between the legs of her little sister. And Lydia will be a far livelier ride than Anne could ever be, I am sure.

He settled himself very near to Lydia and answered her questions charmingly. "Lady Catherine de Bourgh of Rosings Park is an old family friend. She asked me to help her with some urgent matter. That was why I had to leave the army in Meryton without taking proper leave from you. Will you ever forgive me?" He grasped her hand and raised it near his lips.

Lydia had never had such a handsome man paying undivided attention to her before. Flattered, she leaned forward and replied, "Certainly family members can be most troublesome. I forgive you."

He smiled and kissed her hand. His tongue-tip stuck out slightly, just grazing her knuckles.

"My word, you have the softest skin, Miss Lydia!" He raised his head, and his mouth was suddenly close to hers. "I wager that your lips are even softer. Many a gentleman must be willing to die, just to have a taste of them."

Glorying in the compliment, Lydia replied smugly, "Perhaps two and twenty of them have begged to taste my lips, but I am no silly girl. I do not allow just anyone to kiss me there."

"What sort of man might hope to win that privilege, then?"

"He must be tall."

"Indeed."

"And he must be handsome. Nothing like my cousin Mr. Collins."

"Ah! Then may I hope to apply for the privilege, Miss Lydia?"

"Not yet."

"Whyever not?"

"How can I be sure you will not simply kiss and run?"

"Rest assured, I shall be in the neighbourhood for several more days. Then I shall return to Derbyshire. A friend is setting me up to work for a lawyer there. It is time that I begin to think about establishing a family. After all, I shall be ten and thirty tomorrow."

Delighted that he had shared his life plan with her, Lydia leaned closer and kissed him on the cheek. "Oh, happy birthday!"

But instead of looking pleased, he pulled a long face. "That is not fair, Miss Lydia. I want a different sort of birthday kiss."

"On my lips?"

"On the softest skin you have, my dear."

What is the harm of giving him some privileges? He wants to have a family soon and he is so handsome. Ha! Perhaps I shall be the first to get married. So decided, Lydia nodded her permission.

But instead of simply kissing her on the lips, Wickham used his seductive skills to the fullest, and kissed other soft skin upon her. With a combination of sweet talk and tender lips, *PickyWickly* completed another angelic duty in the woods of Rosings Park, not long thereafter, tempted the mortal Miss Lydia Bennet to trade her virtue for the pleasures of the flesh.

***

Inside the guest chamber at the parsonage, Elizabeth was awakened by an application of smelling salts. The doctor soon declared her fine except for being overly tired. Darcy felt guilty once again for keeping her in his bed the whole of the night before, but not guilty enough to let her go. Once the doctor left, he applied to Mr. Bennet again. "Sir, do we have your permission to wed?"

Mr. Bennet looked at the young man who sat by his daughter's bedside, holding her hand, seeming totally besotted with her. After a final moment of reflection, Mr. Bennet nodded solemnly and stated, "Yes, and I shall be happy to call you a son."

Mr. Darcy rose and shook hands with him. "Thank you Mr. Bennet. I shall protect and care for her with all my heart. May we have the wedding by the end of the week?"

"What? Why the rush? Is there anything amiss here?"

"My aunt's servants were involved in our disappearance from London. We do not wish to have to explain to everyone about the night we spent together. For the sake of Miss Bennet's reputation, I think we should wed as promptly as possible. If our families and friends question the rush, Elizabeth can simply tell them again that we have had an understanding since her stay at Netherfield."

Mr. Bennet, seeing his daughter turn a fetching shade of pink, had to agree that not everyone would believe the account of Mrs. Collins's presence during the period of the kidnapping. "Very well then," he agreed.

Elizabeth reached out to him. "Father, may I have a word in private with Mr. Darcy before we tell Mother and the others?"

"Of course. I shall step outside for a few moments."

When Mr. Bennet left the room, Darcy was prepared for a dressing down from his angel, regarding the way in which he had forced her to agree to the marriage. He sat down by her side and held her hands again, resigned to his fate. But before he could utter a word, she drew a deep breath and revealed the crux of the matter to him quite simply. "Mr. Darcy, as an angel, I have been told that I am incapable of bearing a child. We cannot – must not – marry, because I cannot give you an heir." She looked at him squarely, clearly braced to accept the sad news that he was ending the engagement.

Emotions of shock, anger and sadness passed through him but he swallowed them down. She was the most important thing in the world to him. "Then we shall marry without delay and make the most of the time we have together. Georgiana can beget the Darcy's heir. Perhaps we can even raise her second son as our own."

Tears ran down her face as she whispered, "You truly love me enough to accept my...flaw?"

"I love you, deeply ardently, utterly." A tear ran down his cheek as he lowered his head to kiss her tenderly on the lips. "And that is all the more true now that I know that you refused to marry me only for my own good. How can I not love you? And you do not have any flaw." He kissed her again. "In my eyes, you are perfect."

Then he took out his handkerchief to wipe away her tears and his own. "Now, smile, my angel, or your father will think I have mistreated you already. I am happy I can command you to do whatever I want."

She had not known that he could be so teasing. She chuckled through the last of her tears and smacked his arm. "I should not have told you that."

"Yes, I fear it was a major tactical error, my angelic love-slave." And he kissed her tenderly again, before asking Mr. Bennet to rejoin them.

***

When the news of their engagement was announced to the guests and family at the parsonage, everyone there seemed astonished. Mrs. Collins pulled Elizabeth to one side and said frantically, "Lizzy, do you really have to marry him? He flies! Lady Catherine and her daughter are both ill because of what they witnessed. And the three servants were so sacred that they fled the village. Mr. Collins says that Mr. Darcy might be a devil."

"Whatever are you talking about, Maria? I was there last night, too, you know. A gust of wind blew out all of the candles in the church, and Mr. Darcy slipped out then. I certainly did not see him fly. Did you hear Lady Catherine de Bourgh say anything strange about Mr. Darcy last night?"

"No, but ..." Maria bit her lips, clearly unsure what to do.

Elizabeth pressed her advantage. "Does not Mr. Collins say that Lady Catherine is always right?"

Maria nodded her head and agreed.

"Well then, you had best forget what you thought you saw and what Mr. Collins told you. After all, Mr. Darcy is Lady Catherine's nephew. If he proved to be a devil, it would mean that she must be a devil, too." She patted Maria's arm in reassurance. "Mr. Darcy is a good man and I am happy that he offered for me."

On the other side of the room, Colonel Fitzwilliam pulled Mr. Darcy aside and asked him about the hasty marriage.

"Did you compromise the lady?" the Colonel asked in hushed, sober tones. "I thought she said that Mrs. Collins was with her nearly all the time, during the kidnapping. The young woman has no fortune and no connection. Is that truly what you want? Will it not affect Georgiana's future chances, as well?"

"I am a gentleman," Darcy replied, "and she is a gentleman's daughter. In that sense, we are equal. Georgiana and I do not need more wealth and status to advance our happiness." Mr. Darcy squared his shoulders and said firmly, "I would be quite willing to forgo my fortune and connection for a lifetime with her. You will understand, one day, when you find someone who truly completes you."

The serious discussion was disrupted by Mrs. Bennet's exclamations when she learned about the date of the wedding.

"The end of the week? Impossible! This cannot be done!" Mrs. Bennet protested. Only after her husband explained the reason to her did she finally agree. "Well, then, we have so much to do. Where is Lydia? We must return to Longbourn this instant."

Lydia dashed into the room at that moment and flung herself onto a chair. "La, I am so tired!"

"Where have you been?" Mr. Bennet asked.

"I went for a walk in the Park." She smiled smugly. "I like it here, Maria. I like it very much."

"That is of no account," her mother countered unsympathetically, "for we are leaving immediately. Lizzy has agreed to marry Mr. Darcy at the end of the week, and so we must get back to Longbourn to make the wedding preparations. Make haste, girl. How fortunate that we have not unpacked yet!"

"But I do not *want* to go!" Lydia stamped her foot. "Why can I not simply stay here with Maria? Mama, please!"

"It is too late to travel today, but we will return to Longbourn tomorrow," Mr. Bennet announced. "You may come back here with Mary after Lizzy's wedding, if Mrs. Collins agrees. Mr. Darcy, will you accompany us tomorrow?"

"But he..." Lydia's face reddened, and she stamped her foot again.

Mr. Bennet gave her a quelling glare, but instead of remaining silent, she said, "Maria, can we talk?" She then dragged Mrs. Collins out of the room, not even allowing her to properly excuse herself to the other guests.

CHAPTER ELEVEN

Mr. Darcy scowled at Lydia's retreating form, feeling that he should ask her something, but he was unable to pin down what it was about her words and manner that so concerned him before she and Mrs. Collins left the room.

"Mr. Darcy?" Mr. Bennet asked again. "Will you join us tomorrow to Hertfordshire?"

"My apologies, sir." Darcy turned his attention back to the people in the room. "I shall need to travel to London to obtain the special licence and the settlement papers. But here is a thought – perhaps we might all return to London for two days so that Elizabeth can buy her trousseau before we return to Hertfordshire. I am confident that it would please Mr. Bingley to open Netherfield Park for the wedding reception, and to host the guests from my family who wish to attend."

"Oh, Lizzy! What an honour! To have your wedding reception at the grand ballroom in Netherfield. I still remember watching as you danced with Mr. Darcy there. Is that where you charmed him?" Mrs. Bennet exclaimed.

Elizabeth blushed, mortified. *Mother is still Mother!* She thought despairingly. But Mr. Darcy understood her, and unbent so far as to take her hand and offer her a kiss. "Mrs. Bennet, I confess that I have been in love with your daughter since she refused to dance with me at Sir Williams's."

"That early? How romantic! Well, Lizzy has always been impertinent, so it is good that you do not mind it. Oh, and I shall need to talk to Pastor Warwick about the wedding ceremony. And instruct Hill about the reception! My word, there is so much to be done, and I cannot be at two places at the same time," Mrs. Bennet said in happy agitation, fanning her face with the handkerchief. "Whatever shall I do?"

"Calm yourself, Fanny." Mr. Bennet said. "I shall travel with Lizzy to London. Magdalene will help her buy whatever she needs. Meanwhile, you shall take Lydia back to Longbourn and prepare for the wedding."

"No, no," Mrs. Bennet exclaimed, rejecting his plan, "I have been looking forward to marrying off my daughters for many years. I should be the one helping her to choose the dress. You go back to Longbourn with Lydia. Lizzy, we will have to find a modiste who is willing to dress you in a day! What an impossible task!"

Mr. Darcy intervened. "Mrs. Bennet, I shall speak with my sister's modiste. Madam Bouvard is the modiste to Colonel Fitzwilliam's mother, Lady Matlock, as well. I am quite certain that she will be eager to accommodate Miss Elizabeth's needs, for her service to our family is of long standing. And I believe that both of you should stay at Darcy House while you are in London so that you can see what should be altered there to prepare for Miss Elizabeth's arrival after the wedding ceremony. Perhaps your eldest daughter can join you as well." Mr. Darcy said to his future mother. In his mind, he said to Elizabeth, *It is just as well that your father is not coming. I suspect that your mother will be a less strict chaperone. I do not intend to sleep without you ever again.*

Insatiable man! Elizabeth's face turned a shade rosier, and she was about to retort when, instead, her mother exclaimed, "Oh, Lizzy, how lucky are you! Dressed by Her Ladyship's modiste. Of course we shall stay at Mr. Darcy's townhouse."

"Madam, if all of the immediate issues are settled, may I occupy my cousin's time, for now?" Colonel Fitzwilliam inquired. He was eager to draw Mr. Darcy away so that his cousin might calm himself, apart from his alluring fiancée. "Lady Catherine is currently indisposed, and so I need Darcy's assistance in working out the arrangements with the steward. I shall return him to you by tomorrow morning, to escort Miss Bennet and yourself back to London."

"Of course," Mrs. Bennet said before Mr. Darcy could protest. "It is most unfortunate that we cannot see the magnificent Rosings, which Mr. Collins described to us many times. But now that Lizzy will be married to your cousin, I am sure we shall have many chances to stay there in the future."

Colonel Fitzwilliam bowed and hastily dragged Mr. Darcy out of the parsonage before he could even say a proper goodbye to his beloved. Not to be thwarted, Mr. Darcy called out in his mind to Elizabeth: *I shall call for you when I am finished. Fly to me then.*

***

In the grand bedchamber at Rosings, Mr. Darcy paced as he waited for his beloved to arrive. He knew himself to be out of temper, deeply annoyed and frustrated by the attitude that both his cousin and Mr. Collins had taken towards his betrothal.

Although the Colonel agreed that Elizabeth was quite handsome, he was not yet sufficiently well-acquainted with her to fully appreciate her wit, liveliness and attraction. He had been favorably impressed by her relations in London, but her mother and youngest sister were loud and impetuous, clearly without proper breeding. On those grounds, he spent almost an hour trying to persuade Mr. Darcy to reconsider the match.

Mr. Darcy listened as patiently as he could take, then steadfastly extolled Elizabeth's character and virtue to his cousin. In the end, however, his powers of description fell short, and the Colonel would not agree to support Mr. Darcy when he informed Lord Matlock of his impending marriage.

Directly after this frustrating interlude, Mr. Darcy was harassed by Mr. Collins. The clergyman had learned of the engagement from his wife, and he begged Mr. Darcy to rescind his decision.

"Mr. Darcy, my esteemed patron Lady Catherine de Bourgh would never allow this if she could voice her concern now!" Mr. Collins wailed.

"I am master of my own. I allow no one to interfere in my affairs," Mr. Darcy said coldly, and attempted to walk away from the obnoxious man, with the Colonel following close behind.

"But Her Ladyship will petition the Archbishop to forbid such a union. And what a dreadful way to treat the fragile Miss Anne de Bourgh!" Mr. Collins continued, chasing after Mr. Darcy to further argue his case. "I cannot help but feel that she has been most heartlessly ill-used. That esteemed young woman has waited all her life to become your bride, and now she is to be cast aside for a woman ten times below her in consequence?"

Mr. Darcy replied through gritted teeth, "That is all Lady Catherine's doing. I have attempted to dissuade her of such an aspiration for some years, now. At any rate, this is a family affair, a private matter, and I demand that you desist."

"But what can be done to salvage Miss de Bourgh's reputation if you take such a course? Where is your honour, sir? Where is your sense of duty to your family?" When Darcy refused to reply, Mr. Collins drew himself up stiffly and pointed an accusing finger. "You must be possessed by an evil spirit, to even consider serving my esteemed patroness and her daughter in such a manner, especially when they are indisposed! I declare, you will be punished if you continue towards this undesirable liaison. " By now, Mr. Collins was shouting at the top of his voice, and even snatched Darcy's arm to prevent his angry retreat.

Mr. Darcy struggled, trying to dislodge the grip of the overwrought man. Well-intentioned, Colonel Fitzwilliam interfered, trying to separate the two, but in the middle of the struggle the clergyman, breaking away from the Colonel, stumbled against a pillar which supported a massive and expensive vase. Toppling from its perch, the vase landed on Collins's head, knocking him unconscious and shattering into pieces.

Shaken, Mr. Darcy straightened his coat and looked down at the injured man. The doctor was summoned to attend to yet another person at the grand estate.

***

By the time Colonel Fitzwilliam and Mr. Darcy had finished consulting with Lady Catherine's steward and had dined, Mr. Darcy was exhausted. He called out for Elizabeth, looking forward eagerly to spending the night in the arms of his beloved.

He only stopped his pacing when he could finally see a wisp of white flying his way. It was truly amazing to see Elizabeth with her wings fully extended, flying over the formal garden and descending to enter through his window. When she had landed safely in his bedchamber, he greeted her with a passionate kiss.

"I have missed you desperately," Mr. Darcy said when he finally ended the kiss.

She hid her wings and traced her fingers along his cheek. "You look tired. Have you had a hard day? And what is this that I heard from Maria about Mr. Collins having an accident?"

"The injury was no fault of mine. He was like a man possessed, demanding that I end our engagement and honour Lady Catherine's wish. The doctor has seen to him. He will mend. Could we please speak no more of him?" He drew her to sit on the bed. "I would far rather spend this time on us." Lowering his head, he nuzzled her neck.

Elizabeth's heart beat faster at his amorous gesture, but she grasped his broad shoulders and tried to push him away from her. "First, by your leave, I need to discuss a detail concerning the settlement."

Mr. Darcy stopped his kiss. "You have no need to worry about the settlement. I shall take fine care of your sisters, in the event of your father's death."

"That is most generous of you, but you misunderstand me," Elizabeth replied. "I would like you to consult with your lawyer and have him add some written confirmation – or would it be a declaration – from me, to explain my possible …sudden departure in the event of …"

He wrapped his arm tightly around her and kissed her with an air of desperation, pausing only long enough to gasp, "I do not want to talk about you leaving for Heaven, either."

Blinded by his lustful ministration, she responded, kiss for kiss. When he exposed her creamy breasts and suckled her nipples into taut, ruby peaks, she pulled his shirt off and gripped his strong, muscular back with avid force.

His frenzied squeezing and kneading of her bosom made her moan aloud. As she insinuated her fingers within the upper border of his breeches and rubbed his toned bottom, he lowered her onto the bed and traced kisses along her abdomen. With ardent care, he pressed his parted lips to the gauzy fabric of her gown and used his talented tongue to create a wet, hot painting on her body while her impatient hands moved to skillfully unbutton his breeches.

Deftly, he divested her of her dress, revealing her glorious naked form for his intense survey. But when he tried to lower his head to taste her folds, she gripped his shoulders again and said tentatively, blushing, "I believe I would like to taste *you*, this time. Will you teach me?"

His eyes widened at her daring request, and his arousal, already substantial, grew even harder. Stripping off his breeches with haste, he lay back on the bed and said, in a voice which he could not hold quite steady, "This is … new to me as well." He held her hand and rubbed his thumb along her palm. "I am yours to explore as you will."

A shiver flashed through her body, and she felt a heated wetness gather at her apex. She drew a deep breath, letting her gaze rove along his neck, his solid torso, his lean, hard abdomen, before coming to rest finally on his magnificent shaft.

Lowering her head, Elizabeth kissed the springing curls of his bush. As her lips neared his shaft, she saw from the corner of her eye that he was gripping the bed sheet tightly.

His proud member seemed to grow larger still, and his masculine scent flooded her nostrils, making her dizzy with desire. Kneeling at his side, she braced one hand on his thigh and the other on the mattress, to steady herself. She pressed her lips to the base of his shaft, kissing her way slowly up his hot, tight-stretched rod, and felt him squirm, moaning.

She raised her head and looked at him. His eyes were half shut, his teeth set in his lower lip, his chest heaving up and down in rapid rhythm.

Emboldened, she licked his manhood from base to top. The salty, faintly woody taste of his skin was addictive. She could not resist kissing the tip, then saluting the velvety skin there with a delicate lick.

His pulsing shaft greeted her moist lips with a mind of its own. His lower body jerked, his hips rising as he thrust into her small mouth.

The sensation of taking his arousal into her mouth was beyond words. It felt like swallowing a hot hard stone column that was yet slick and silky. The muscles inside her mouth and her tongue were bombarded with heat, scent, flavour, and vibration. The sound of his moans added to the spectrum of stimulation, all claiming her attention.

She felt his member swell even further, and was surprised by his sudden movement to push her away. Her mouth mourned the loss of his core, but he quickly rolled her onto her back and invaded her entrance with a strong thrust.

He put his hands down on either side of her, to bear his weight as he pounded into her with maddened speed. She welcomed him, wet and ready to receive his every thrust, her body much more fully capable of enveloping him than her mouth had been. She parted her legs more widely for him, granting him deeper access, her core shaken by his movement, vibration and friction.

In less than a minute, he groaned with ecstasy and spent himself inside of her, without having taken her to her peak. Drawing her up to enfold her in his arms, he rolled onto his back, carrying her along so that she was newly positioned on top on him. Then, after trailing his fingers down her spine and over the fine cheeks of her bottom, he brought his hands around to the front and used his blunt, agile thumbs to explore her damp folds, rubbing and chafing at the tiny nub hidden there.

Elizabeth was sent off the edge by this last ministration. Shivering, trembling, shuddering like a woman possessed, she moaned in ecstasy as she convulsed, her secret muscles tightening around his shaft, a new experience that gave them both extreme pleasures.

Then she sank down upon him, exhausted, and they both slipped into a deep sleep, cuddling each other close.

***

Early next morning, Mr. Darcy commanded Lady Catherine's barouche to take Mr. Bennet and the reluctant Lydia back to Longbourn. She wanted to stay in Kent or, failing that, at least to go to London to shop. But her mother, for the first time, did not yield to her demand. Mrs. Bennet did not want her youngest daughter to distract her from the important duty of preparing Elizabeth. As a result, Lydia left for Hertfordshire extremely displeased.

That same morning, Mr. Darcy's carriage conveyed Elizabeth and her mother to London, while he and Colonel Fitzwilliam accompanied them on horseback.

Elizabeth had observed the cool demeanor of the Colonel towards her mother and herself, and she decided to talk to her mother about it. "Mama, I remember you saying that you do not like to travel on long journeys. I was astonished to see you at Hunsford." Elizabeth began.

"Oh, hang my dislikes! My little girl was kidnapped and could have been lost to me again. What would you have had me do, languish in my bedchamber and complain about my nerves while I wait for your absent-minded father to remember to relate the news to me? I was determined to do no such thing."

"Again?" Elizabeth echoed. "Had I been lost to you before?"

"Umh..." Mrs. Bennet turned her face to the window, avoided her daughter's enquiring gaze.

Elizabeth took her mother's hand. "Mama...will you not tell me how you found me in Derbyshire?" she urged gently.

Mrs. Bennet turned back to look at her daughter with wide eyes. "Who told you about that?" Tears welled in her eyes as she said, in an agitated voice, "We cannot have other people knowing about this. I do not care if you *are* a foundling. You are my Lizzy, and I shall not allow anyone to look down on you because of it!"

Elizabeth, touched by this vehement defence, embraced her mother. "Thank you, Mama. I learned about it from a trusted source. He would not tell anyone."

Mrs. Bennet scowled, as if starting to work her way through all of the men with whom her daughter had recently been acquainted. Then her frown eased. "Ah, Mr. Darcy told you? He must have been only a few years old himself at the time. Did he see me when I found you by the pond? Magdalene told me that his estate of Pemberley is only a few miles from Lambton. And I found you a few miles from that little village, so it must have been near to his estate. He really is a good man, to overlook the mystery of your birth and still offer for you."

Elizabeth nodded her head, deciding not explain the truth to her mother. After all, she could not tell her about the Lost Angel Commissioner. "Yes, Mr. Darcy is the best of men, and I love him dearly. So, you found me by a pond?"

"Yes." Her features softened. "Oh my, you cannot imagine how ecstatic I was when I found you. Your father, Jane and I were staying at your Uncle Gardiner's place. He stayed in Cheshire at the time. My own lovely, adorable Lizzy died in her sleep without warning, a few days after her birth. I hope you never experience the piercing pain of losing someone you loved so much." She stifled a sob. "All I could remember were the smiles, the kicks, the sweet, cooing voice of my baby Lizzy…and then the sudden cold, grey-tinged skin of her dead body when I found her not breathing, one morning. I blamed myself for not checking on her during the night. I did not eat or talk for a whole week afterwards."

"Oh, that is so very tragic!" Elizabeth said and squeezed Mrs. Bennet's hand. "But it was not your fault."

"My heart was heavy, from that horrible morning on. Then we journeyed back to Hertfordshire and stopped near Lambton. When I found you, without a stitch of clothing, out by the pond, Thomas said that whoever left you there did not want to be found. You were crying, at first, but then you gave us the most brilliant smile, reminding me so much of my Lizzy that I could not think of calling you by any other name." She returned Elizabeth's gesture. "I felt alive again. My Lord gave me a second chance, and I vowed that I would not be negligent, and that I would guard you well, this time."

"Mama, you were never negligent. It was just an accident."

"I know you resent all my nervous arguments about you going off for a walk alone, or climbing a tree, or my fluttering about marrying you off to a rich man. But I just want the best for you. Sometimes, when you left the house, I would worry about all of the accidents that could claim your life. And I know you are the smartest of all my girls, but if your father were to die before you married, I could not bear to see your spirit crushed by becoming a governess, or having to marry a man of low birth who has no wit."

Elizabeth hugged her mother again. "Mama, I am sorry to have doubted you in the past."

"All is well now, my dear." She returned her daughter's embrace. "Did I not discourage that silly, condescending Mr. Collins away from both you and Jane? Now that you have secured such a well-bred, intelligent, wealthy man, I am confident that he will take good care of you and all your sisters, should Mr. Bennet meet his destiny. Your husband-to-be seems a bit dull and arrogant to me, but I can see that he is besotted with you. I shall try my best to act and speak with more decorum ... especially with regard to his grand houses and his strong, masculine figure."

"Mama!"

"What? You think I did not notice how your eyes followed his pert derriere as he climbed atop that big horse, just now?" She smiled. "It is good to desire your husband. And you must always keep him interested in you. Then life will be blissful for you both. I regret that I have not been doing as I preach. I have been too busy worrying about the future of my girls to attend properly to the care of your father, but I can and shall change! The next time that I am silly or loud, you must pinch my arm to remind me of my resolve."

"I cannot very well do that in a room full of people. But I *shall* consider nudging you discreetly with my elbow." At that, mother and daughter burst out laughing.

During the second half of the journey, it started to rain, and so the gentlemen joined them in the carriage. Mrs. Bennet immediately acted upon her vow to improve her manners in order to impress her beloved daughter's future family. The vivacious, lively young Fanny who had so bedazzled Mr. Bennet many years ago returned, and she was able to charm Colonel Fitzwilliam with her questions. Further impressed by the witty remarks Elizabeth occasionally made, the Colonel finally conceded to himself that the Bennet ladies might prove to be a lovely set of relations. Nevertheless, Elizabeth did need to nudge her mother's elbow from time to time, when Mrs. Bennet's old silliness threatened to emerge again.

What has happened to your mother? Mr. Darcy mind talked to Elizabeth.

I do not know what you mean,

She is acting much like you, teasing and sweet to my cousin, instead of sounding like a ...

Do not venture there!

I am sorry, my dear. I am just happy that Richard seems to warm to you and your family now. He had reservations about our hasty plans to marry, yesterday.

I know. He was cool to us earlier, Elizabeth said.

Although I shall brook no objection to our union, I still hope that the Matlocks will sanction it. Richard is a joint guardian of Georgiana, and I do love my uncle and aunt. It will be good to have their blessing.

Your cousin can influence his parents?

Richard is his mother's favourite. A good word from him will go a long way towards gaining Lady Matlock's approval for us.

And I, of course, will do whatever I can for you, my demanding ward. Shall I abandon you and set my mind on charming your cousin, as well?

Do not dare. Your charms are reserved only for me!

The voiced and silent banter went on in the carriage during the damp journey. By the time the carriage drew to a halt at Gracechurch Street, Colonel Fitzwilliam had volunteered to request that his mother invite the Bennet ladies to breakfast and go shopping with them the next day, if she did not have a prior engagement.

Mr. Darcy could not wipe the smile from his face as he introduced Mrs. Bennet and the two Bennet sisters to Georgiana, and then saw his cousin off from his townhouse with a round of warm thanks.

CHAPTER TWELVE

On first seeing the magnificent Darcy House, Mrs. Bennet could not repress her oohs and ahs. Elizabeth, however, no longer felt embarrassed by her mother's genuine expressions of admiration. She simply smiled and engaged herself in talking with Miss Darcy.

After light refreshments, Mr. Darcy left the ladies to prepare the settlement and to obtain the special licence.

Before he went out, Elizabeth excused herself from the party and wrote a letter to her parents. She entrusted the sealed letter to her fiancé, asking that it be given to the lawyer. In it, she told them the reasons for her sudden disappearance, should such an event occur, and asked them to assist Mr. Darcy in dispelling any rumours or gossip that might arise. The letter would be part of the settlement, only to be opened at Darcy's request.

Mr. Darcy was most reluctant to be the bearer of such correspondence but, in the end, Elizabeth persuaded him.

She then spent a pleasant afternoon with Miss Darcy and toured the townhouse in greater detail. She was happy with the existing elegant décor and furnishings, and did not anticipate requiring any change to them.

As evening fell, Mr. Darcy and Colonel Fitzwilliam joined the ladies during the dinner. The Colonel, they soon learned, brought good news. Not only would Lady Matlock invite them to breakfast at the Earl's townhouse and join them at the modiste on the morrow, she was also planning to attend the ball at Lady Barrymore's, that night, and she had used her influence to expand the invitation to include Mr. Darcy and the Bennet ladies.

"What better way to dispel the gossip of the ton regarding a hasty marriage by attacking with a united front?" Colonel Fitzwilliam recounted his mother's words.

But the news sent Mrs. Bennet into hyperventilation. "My girls do not have a ball gown! Who can take care of Lizzy's hair here? Their shoes are all wrong! Their complexion will be ruined for the ball after a busy day of shopping!"

Colonel Fitzwilliam dragged his cousin away from the ladies' presence, the better to let them strategise. It wasn't until midnight that he finally took his leave. After seeing him off, Mr. Darcy slipped into Elizabeth's room and snuggled behind her charming but exhausted form. He was happy simply to hold her tight and let her sleep, counting every minute of being with her as a minute well-spent.

***

"My dear, is it not risky to take these unknown women to Lady Barrymore's ball?" Lord Matlock asked his wife as she prepared to welcome their nephew's fiancée for breakfast. "They may behave like savages, making Darcy – and us with him – the laughing stock of the ton."

"Desperate time calls for desperate measures," Lady Matlock replied. "Your sister's stupid action effectively sealed Fitzwilliam's honor with that woman. But Richard's praise of the Bennets has encouraged me to rethink the issue."

"Do you mean to say that you agree with Richard that we should accept this country lass with open arms, simply because Darcy is besotted with her?"

"I have not decided yet. More to the point, if she makes a spectacle of Fitzwilliam tonight, surely he will rethink marrying her. The wedding is arranged for the end of the week.

We need to shock him. He will not change his mind simply because we request that he do so. I can weather the storm of one night easily enough, in service to such a necessary goal."

"I hope you are right, my dear. At any rate, I shall take Darcy to the club today and give him some advice about his choice," Lord Matlock said.

"Just be careful not to anger him. You know how stubborn he can be. Perhaps the lady and her family are as wonderful as Richard claims. After all, Fitzwilliam is a fastidious young man. You and I, as well as the mothers of the ton, have been parading women, young and mature, pretty and plain, smart and dull, in front of him for the past several years. Despite our best efforts, he has never shown the least interest in marrying any of them. I do not think he would be besotted just because of some woman's wiles and allurements. There must be something special about her. Perhaps all shall be fine tonight. Perhaps I can even frighten the young woman away, this morning," Lady Matlock said with a confident smile.

"You frighten her?" Lord Matlock shook his head. "You are far too soft-hearted when it comes to Darcy. Ah well. You must do what you can, and I will do my part, as well. Then we shall see who achieves the most satisfactory result."

"And what result would that be?"

"Whatever is best for Darcy. If the lady make him truly happy, I shall not mind that she has little in the way of fortune or connections. He has been alone for too long."

"But of course."

With that, they went down to welcome their nephew and his intended's family. Colonel Fitzwilliam was there to introduce them. Darcy left reluctantly to the club with his uncle and cousin.

Lady Matlock was awed by the beauty of the blond lady whom she thought was Darcy's intended at first. But in fact, that was Miss Jane Bennet. Her Ladyship then turned her attention to Miss Elizabeth, and was surprised by Darcy's choice.

Although quite handsome, Miss Elizabeth could not rival her sister's beauty, nor that of many of the ton's women who had sought Darcy's attention for some time. Lady Matlock's interest was piqued. It was unfortunate that her husband had dragged Darcy away for a manly tête-à-tête. She would have liked to watch his interaction with the young lady in question. For the moment, Lady Matlock made up her mind to act more like her sister, Lady Catherine de Bourgh.

"Mrs. Bennet, Miss Bennet and Miss Elizabeth, you are welcome." Lady Matlock acknowledged the ladies. "Georgiana, it is good to see you."

"Thank you, aunt," Georgiana replied.

"Your Ladyship, it is our great honour to be your guest," Mrs. Bennet said. "We are also thrilled to have been offered the use of your modiste's services, later on."

"It is unfortunate that the whole affair is so rushed," Her Ladyship said with a scowl, and waited for their reaction. She could see that Miss Bennet seemed nervous over the direction of the conversation, but Miss Elizabeth only arched her eyebrows and continued to divide her attention between her mother and Georgiana.

"My sentiments exactly, Your Ladyship," Mrs. Bennet agreed. "But Mr. Darcy and my husband said that no one would believe that Maria – the wife of Lady Catherine de Bourgh's parson – was there to chaperone Lizzy when she spent the night with Mr. Darcy in the hands of the highwaymen."

"Mama, remember, they were not highwaymen. They were simply Lady Catherine's overeager servants," Elizabeth said. "Your Ladyship, I am sorry if the timing of our wedding causes your uneasiness. I did attempt to persuade Mr. Darcy to wait and see, but he was most insistence."

"You are not eager to marry my brother?" Georgiana exclaimed, astonished. She had never met a single eligible woman who did not wish to marry her rich, handsome brother.

"Or perhaps she is playing *hard to get*," Lady Matlock added on purpose as she tore up a piece of bread with force.

"It is *hard to get* such delicious chocolate in Hertfordshire, Your Ladyship," Elizabeth replied equably, then turned to Georgiana. "Indeed, your brother is the finest of men, handsome, intelligent and, of course, extremely wealthy. But I must confess that the prospect of marrying him did rather frighten me, at first."

"Why did you not tell me so before, Lizzy?" Mrs. Bennet asked with concern. "I would have never agreed with your father's wishes if I had known it."

"But you should have known, Mama. Did he not once say I was not handsome enough to tempt him?" Elizabeth reminded her with a smile. "I fear he may adjudge me 'not handsome enough' again soon, and abandon me after a day of marriage."

"Oh that!" Mrs. Bennet burst out laughing. "You are determined to vex me with your drollery."

Jane smiled and shook her head. Seeing the confused look on Miss Darcy's face, she said, "Georgiana, do not be alarmed. Lizzy's favourite pastime is to jest and make us laugh."

"I am relieved," Georgiana said, smiling too, "because surely that could not be true. My brother would never have behaved so rudely."

"To ridicule people of great wit is not a good employment of time," Lady Matlock said, and frowned, only to find that she was surprised by the Bennet ladies' reaction to her open displeasure. They did not appear intimidated by her position and wealth, for they continued to jest as usual. And they seemed to have gained Georgiana's confidence. Her niece was using both young ladies' Christian names, and they seemed to include her at all times in their conversation. Most unusual! Most scheming women would have invested their energy by engaging Lady Matlock's attention, in such a situation.

"Georgiana, I am sorry to disappoint you. Mama and Jane said I jested only because they did not believe my fear of your brother's abandonment. But he did once tell Mr. Bingley that I was not handsome enough to tempt him to dance, when I first met him at the Meryton Assembly. He has since begged prettily for my forgiveness, and he is kind enough to praise my beauty almost every time he sees me, in recompense," Elizabeth said, continuing to shock Georgiana with her revelations. Then she turned her attention to Lady Matlock. "Actually, Your Ladyship, your nephew once said something similar to me. He observed that the wisest and best of men's actions could still be rendered ridiculous by a person whose first object in life was to joke. I hope I may never ridicule what is wise and good, though I did accuse him, at the time, of being proud and vain."

"Proud! Vain!" Lady Matlock said. She could see why Darcy was besotted with this girl. She was lively and natural, and she could hold her opinion against anyone. "What made you say such a thing to him?"

"He nearly would not talk or dance with anyone when he first arrived in Hertfordshire." Elizabeth explained. "We all mistook his actions for pride and vanity. But I understand now that he had some worries about … his estate that made him behave most differently at the time. Of course, all of that shall be forgotten now. I shall tell everyone that I invented the story of his slight at the Assembly. As a result, Mr. Darcy will be applauded and worshiped like a saint for rescuing a Bennet daughter from spinsterhood."

At that, everyone burst out laughing. Even Lady Matlock could not suppress a smile.

"Lizzy!" Mrs. Bennet chastised, but she, too, was beaming.

By the end of the day, Lady Matlock admitted that Mr. Darcy had chosen well. Although Mrs. Bennet could be silly and loud at times, Lady Matlock did like her genuine concern for the welfare of her daughters much better than Lady

Catherine's single-minded pursuit of the Darcy wealth for her own gain.

She noticed that their relations in trade were mentioned with fondness. And she recalled that Richard had told her that they were well-bred people with wit and manner.

During the appointment at the modiste, the Bennet sisters did not choose the most expensive items, even after assurance from Lady Matlock that Mr. Darcy had sanctioned it. They only chose clothes and fabrics that suited their style and taste. They also encouraged Georgiana to try on designs that were slightly more sophisticated than her usual fashion.

Lady Matlock was happy to be able to reassure her grumpy husband – who had had a hard and unrewarding time attempting to persuade Darcy into a rethink – that there was nothing to worry about, concerning the Bennet ladies. They might not wear the very finest gowns, or come with the unparalleled best of connections, but they were intelligent, well-mannered and caring.

***

Inside Lady Barrymore's grand ballroom, a buzz was circulating. Every mama in the ton had been upset by the gossip. The master of Pemberley, one of the most eligible bachelors of the past seven years, had chosen a wife, and she was not someone they knew. The wedding was planned to take place in the next few days, in such a rush that speculation of entrapment had spread like wildfire among the sitting rooms of the London townhouses, that afternoon. Knowing that Lady Barrymore was a good friend of Lady Matlock, many were eager to catch some gossip tonight, should the Matlocks attend.

They were not prepared for Mr. Darcy to make an appearance himself, especially with the lady in question on his arm.

"Look at that translucent silk! It is one of the most fashionable fabrics of this season," one onlooker said with envy at the sight of Elizabeth's gown.

"She is not one tenth as handsome as Lady Irving. And the blond sister looks prettier, as well. Does Mr. Darcy have no taste at all?" another said.

"The way those yellow pansies are woven into her hair is pure country style. So out of fashion."

"Her skin is quite coarse. She must have stayed out in the sun for too long. These country misses do not know what is important in their lives."

"Well, I heard the mother was too vulgar to be brought along to the ball tonight, even though she is in town. And they have an uncle in trade, living in Cheapside."

"Tell me, do you think the woman looks as if she is with child?"

"Hmm. She does not look sick…and she is quite light on her feet. No, I would say she is not with child."

"But she glows with happiness. She *must* be with child."

"Her eyes are sly, sizing up every man in the room. Even General Spencer is smitten. I wager she will stray, after the marriage."

Her companion suddenly gasped. "Look at Mr. Darcy!"

"He laughs! Oh, my, he looks even handsomer when he laughs and shows those dimples."

"He never takes his eyes away from that country lass. I fear that all is lost for my Claire."

This was but a tithe of the gossip flying around the ballroom, But Mr. Darcy ignored them all. He was extremely happy to be dancing with his lovely fiancée again.

Indeed, Mr. Darcy's good humour was now fully restored, all thanks to Elizabeth. Agitated in the morning by his uncle's attempt to persuade him to forgo the match, he had then spent a lonely afternoon in the study, waiting for Elizabeth to come home after shopping. His grim demeanor had persisted until just before the bath water was drawn for the ladies. Mrs.

Bennet, fatigued by the events of the past few days, had elected to remain in her bedchamber for the rest of the night, sorry not to be able to attend the ball. Learning of this decision, Mr. Darcy had managed to slip into Elizabeth's room, where he spent the most satisfying and invigorating half-hour with her, in the bath.

Now dancing with his beautiful fiancée in the first set of the night, Darcy gazed at her gorgeous form. As he moved towards her along the dance line, and then around her, he decided to remain silent and engage in mind talk with her. It was more exhilarating and liberating to communicate in that very private way.

That green translucent silk looks beautiful on you, Mr. Darcy said.

Sir, you are disconcertingly well-versed in the delicate fabrics worn by ladies, Elizabeth replied saucily.

I must confess that I like you even better without a stitch of fabric on, but only when we are alone.

Be careful with your thoughts. Many women are hoping for some scandalous event to occur tonight, to make you abandon your choice with me.

Never! But I do want to dance a waltz with you. What a pity that Lady Barrymore did not sanction the scandalous dance.

We have danced the waltz before.

Yes, but it was like a dream to me, at the time. I want to be awake this time, to have your nipples graze against my chest, to hold your small waist and smell your sweet scent as we swirl to the seductive music.

Desist, Fitzwilliam! You have made me all hot and flustered. I will forget the dance steps and trample on your toes soon.

Unfortunately, I must also think of something else, or I will embarrass both you and the ton with my blatant arousal.

Mr. Darcy removed his gaze from Elizabeth's lovely complexion to calm himself, only to see with astonishment that Miss Bingley and Mr. Collins were deep in discussion at the far end of the ballroom.

"What are *they* doing here?" Darcy muttered.

When the dance finished, Mr. Darcy and Elizabeth returned to their party and found that Jane and Colonel Fitzwilliam had introduced Miss Bingley and Mr. Collins to Lord and Lady Matlock.

Mr. Darcy was seething. He had vowed to cut his tie with Bingley's sister completely, after the sleeping draft incident, but he had forgotten to inform Miss Bennet of his decision, due to the kidnapping.

He was even angrier when Mr. Collins asked Elizabeth for the next dance. As the clergyman took his beloved out on the dance floor, Miss Bingley approached, with the obvious intent of obtaining a dance from him. Instead, Mr. Darcy excused himself from the party and moved to the refreshment table. He would rather separate from his party than dance with that vile woman.

"I hope you have recovered from your accident," Elizabeth said. She reflected that Mr. Collins seemed strangely different. He seemed to be able to dance much better than before.

"All is well, and I have come all the way from Kent to instruct you, Lizzybell," he replied, his tone deep and menacing.

Elizabeth nearly missed a step and trampled on his foot. Shaken, she drew in a deep breath and tried to calm her nerves. Elizabeth could hear him clearly but strangely she did not see him open his mouth. *How does he know who I am? How is he able to 'mind-talk' with me as well?*

"Instruct me on what?" She would not admit her angelic status yet but asked her question aloud.

"End your engagement with your ward." He replied in a low voice this time.

"Why should I do as you say?"

"Because, otherwise, his cousin's life will be lost."

"Mr. Darcy's freedom for Colonel Fitzwilliam's life?" she hissed, wary of being overheard by the other dancers.

"No. You misunderstand me. Miss Bingley wants Mr. Darcy. End your engagement with him now and I shall spare Miss de Bourgh's life."

She fought down her nerves, trying to think rationally. "Your argument is most ill-based. Even if I give up Mr. Darcy, he will never offer for Miss Bingley."

"He will do as I say, if he wants to save his cousin."

"You will be put away for threatening Lord Matlock's niece."

Mr. Collins grinned, showing his teeth. "No human can touch me."

"You are an angel, as well?" she asked, not wanting to believe it.

"Low-level angels like you do not know about us at all," he said arrogantly as he surveyed the room with an air of self importance.

Elizabeth's mind was reeling. She needed more information, if she was to have any hope of protecting Mr. Darcy and his cousin. Perhaps Michael could help her. For now, she decided to flatter her odious partner.

"Would you enlighten this ignorant, low-level angel, sir?" she asked, smiling charmingly. "With whom do I have the pleasure of dancing?"

"Well, since you ask so nicely, I am *Corcifa* from *Tartara*, the dark corner at the eastern end of *Himins*. My master, *Baphoma*, is *Zenobie*'s twin who broke away from *Himins* to set up his own sphere. While *Zenobie*'s underlings like you deal with minor rescue and small-scale temptation in this world, we *Assuras* discover the basest of human desires and help them fulfill their most fervent intent."

"*Assuras?*"

"*Assuras* are what people here would call 'demons'."

Elizabeth gasped. "You are a demon? All your life, Mr. Collins?"

"Ah, the unfortunate Mr. Collins departed this world when he was knocked on the head by Colonel Fitzwilliam. As he was most angry with Mr. Darcy at the time of his death, and because I received urgent pleas from Miss Bingley through her herbal doctor, I have taken over his body for the time being."

Her eyes widened. "So you do not negotiate this deal on Mr. Collins's behalf?"

"Far from it. I act for Miss Bingley."

"What did she promise you in exchange?"

"That is between Miss Bingley and myself."

"But what about me? I am supposed to look after my ward. Surely I will be punished by *Zenobie* for allowing Mr. Darcy to marry a woman who bargains with a demon."

"I can give you protection, my dear. Come to *Tartara* with me. We have better wine, better entertainment, more virile immortals and fewer rules than *Himins*. I, the great *Corcifa*, can satisfy your carnal needs far better than that Mr. Darcy." He moved nearer to her in the dance step, and his chest almost grazed across her breasts.

Elizabeth felt nauseated by his closeness. He smelt like moist rotten wood. While she was contemplating how to reply to his proposition, Mr. Collins commanded: "Tomorrow at midnight, bring your fiancé to the graveyard at the back of Meryton Church. There I shall perform the wedding ceremony between Miss Bingley and Mr. Darcy. You have until then to consider seeking my protection, or else risk *Himins's* retribution."

"And Miss de Bourgh?

"Mrs. Collins will travel to Hertfordshire with her. I shall deliver her to you after Miss Bingley's marriage is consummated."

Elizabeth gasped. She could not allow Fitzwilliam to be harmed. Miss Bingley had bargained her soul to a demon. Fitzwilliam would be tainted, too, if he slept with her. Still, to allow herself more time in which to consult Michael, Elizabeth nodded her head as if in agreement with Mr. Collins's demand.

The dance ended, and Mr. Darcy moved in quickly to claim Elizabeth's hand. But Mr. Collins did not release her other hand until after he had bowed and kissed it.

What did the man want? I saw him dancing too near to you just now. How was he able to recover so fast and come to the ball with Bingley's horrible sister? Mr. Darcy asked silently.

Elizabeth did not know how to relate the bad tidings. She shook her head, squeezed his hand hard and replied, *I will come to you room later. We will talk about it then. For now, let us enjoy tonight.*

Mr. Darcy could sense her worry but nodded his head and agreed to wait. Then they did just as she had proposed: they enjoyed the night. He danced only once each with Lady Matlock and Jane; then he spent all of the other dances, as well as supper, with Elizabeth. They did not care where Mr. Collins and Miss Bingley were. They gazed only at each other, and engaged in sweet conversations. Everyone could see that they were besotted with each other. Regardless of any gossip or speculation, the Matlocks were happy that Darcy had found his love.

CHAPTER THIRTEEN

After Mr. Darcy dismissed Wharton, he waited anxiously for his beloved. He knew something grave had happened during her dance with Mr. Collins, something which had dampened her happy countenance throughout the remainder of the evening. He could only hope that it would not affect their wedding.

When Elizabeth finally entered his room via the servant's entrance, he greeted her immediately. "Did Mr. Collins bring bad tidings?" Mr. Darcy asked.

"Do you have a piece of paper?" she requested.

Puzzled, Darcy moved to his desk and took out a sheet of stationery for her.

She sat down at the desk and produced an odd-looking quill. "I need to speak with Michael, the Lost Angel Commissioner. I hope he is willing to appear in front of you because the matter directly concerns you."

Before he could reply, she started writing. Then a puff of smoke by the window drew his gaze, as the high-level angel appeared.

Staring, Mr. Darcy saw him as a man with long blond hair and wide eyes. Drawing in a startled breath, he said, "Good evening to you, the Commissioner."

"Call me Michael. *Himins* is liberal with greeting etiquettes. I see you have won *Lizzybell*'s affection. She no longer protests about you having your wicked way with her, and she joins you in your bedchambers quite willingly."

"Sir, I protest! What I said to you should be kept private." Elizabeth insisted.

"Women! I do not see what is wrong. He lusts after you. You love his passionate love-making and protest only half-heartedly. Indeed, you now lust after him, too. What is there to keep private?" Michael shrugged.

"I requested your presence not for this but for a truly grave matter," she insisted, blushing bright red.

"Well then, I am all ears." Michael moved to sit on the chaise and folded his long legs up. "Do you have a glass of whisky, Darcy?"

"Certainly," Darcy replied.

"NO!" Elizabeth said at the same time. "You cannot waste time drinking now. I met *Corcifa* the demon from *Tartara* tonight."

Michael bolted up from the chaise. "Where?"

"At Lady Barrymore's ball."

"In what form?"

"In my cousin, Mr. Collins's body."

Mr. Darcy gasped upon hearing this exchange. "Does that mean that Mr. Collins is dead?"

"That son of a bitch! I shall get him this time." Michael swore.

"I am relieved," Elizabeth admitted. "He said that no one could touch him."

"I know all of his weaknesses," Michael said. "What did he want from you?"

"He is doing Miss Bingley's bidding. She wants Fitzwilliam to marry her…in exchange for sparing Miss de Bourgh's life."

"What?!" Darcy scowled.

"Damn!" Michael swore again. "Another chance lost. I have been itching to strangle the man."

"You cannot fight him?" she asked, holding Darcy's hand.

"Protecting your ward is your duty, so I cannot interfere," Michael explained.

"But you have only taught me to fly and to generate some winds. Are those skills enough to fight a demon?" She squeezed her beloved's hand more tightly.

Michael took out the little black book from his sleeves, flipped over several pages and then said, "There is no rule against me watching or preparing you to fight the toad."

"I gather that this demon and you do not get on," Mr. Darcy observed.

"Get on? I want to kick his buttocks. Seven years ago, he gave protection to one of the lost angels I had been tracking for some months, right under my nose. My performance card was blackened, and it took me two years to regain my former standing. I could have been a level-one angel by now, were it not for that bloody demon."

"It is good to hear that you want to kick …" Elizabeth began, then amended, "I mean, it is a relief to me that you will assist me in foiling Miss Bingley's scheme. Should we start now? The night is not long."

"So anxious to defend your territory," Michael teased. "I do not see your Mr. Darcy sparing even a glance at that feathered woman. Still, you do not have to worry about *Corcifa*. I am superior to him, in skill and in appearance."

She frowned, looking at him skeptically. She was not prepared to take any chances with regard to Mr. Darcy's safety, but she appeased the angel by nodding her head. "Of course. If we could just begin…"

"You will know soon enough," Michael said. He surveyed the room. "It is too crowded here. We will go to the park nearby, where the learning will begin."

"May I come, too?" Darcy asked hurriedly.

"But people will find it strange that you are alone in the park at this time of the night," Elizabeth warned.

"I excel in fencing. Maybe Michael can teach me how to…eliminate the evil from…the feathered woman, while you take care of the demon."

"A fine idea!" Michael agreed. "I would love to see *Corcifa's* protégé crumble in front of his eyes. And no one will see Mr. Darcy with our angelic clouds surrounding him."

"I am not sure…" Elizabeth bit her lips and turned to Mr. Darcy, "What if Miss Bingley has some devilish power, too? I do not want you to be hurt."

"Oh, spare me such romantic mush." Michael rolled his eyes. "If he cannot fight her, he can always kiss her into submission. That feathered woman would swoon when she tasted your lover boy's lips. Now, come. I do not have the whole night. I shall wait for the two of you in the park."

Mr. Darcy grinned. "Your lover boy? I like this Michael. Wait for me. I shall go and fetch my sword." With that, he ran out of the room, leaving an exasperated Elizabeth behind.

A few short minutes later, Mr. Darcy returned with the sword and his greatcoat to find that his fiancée had changed into a more serviceable dress and was waiting, with her wings spread.

Despite the serious circumstances, he could not hide his smile. He asked with boyish wonder, "Can we fly side by side, this time? I want to see the world under our feet when we fly."

"Just like a boy." Elizabeth shook her head at his excitement and wrapped her right hand around his waist, while he passed his left hand securely around hers. While she concentrated on the park and the intricacies of flying them through the open window, he was tantalised by her sweet scent and the rubbing of one of her wings against his shoulder. After observing the exhilarating sight of the rooftops passing below, he turned his head and suckled her earlobe.

Elizabeth shivered at the warm sensation that cruised through her body, making her lose concentration. They dropped altitude immediately. "Behave when I fly! If I crash, it may well break all your bones," she chastised him, and focused on their destination once again.

Darcy's heart had nearly jumped out of his chest at the sudden drop. He gave her an apologetic glance and turned away again, content to enjoy the wind and the sights of flying instead. However, when they finally drew near Michael at the park and hovered just a foot from the ground, Darcy could not repress the surge of youthful mischief that such an experience had incited in him, and he kissed his angel soundly on the cheek.

The unexpected caress caused her to lose her composure. Stumbling, she lost her footing as she touched down and landed on her backside on the grass, causing him to topple onto her.

"Sorry! Did I crush you?" He rolled away and stood to help her up immediately, still wearing a silly grin on his face.

"That is the most horrible landing I have ever witnessed," Michael laughed, and gave Mr. Darcy a sly glance. "I can see that I must teach you more angelic skills, to better enable you to handle your ward."

Elizabeth glared at both men, while Mr. Darcy, barely suppressing his smile, urged the Lost Angel Commissioner to begin his lessons.

Michael first talked about the demon's strengths and weaknesses. Then he demonstrated a few moves and tricks for Elizabeth. While she was practicing, he told Mr. Darcy where to find the weakest point of a human possessed by the demon, what kind of method he should use, and the effect that it would have.

The angelic lesson continued for an hour and a half. Michael was pleased by Elizabeth and Darcy's quick understanding, but Elizabeth wanted to practice more. While she was busy repeating the moves, Mr. Darcy pulled Michael aside and handed him a flask of his best whisky, which he had kept hidden in the pocket of his greatcoat.

"Ah! How did you know I would be thirsty by now?" Michael inhaled the pure aroma of the human drink, then gulped down a big mouthful. "This is much better than what we have in *Himins*."

Mr. Darcy linked his hands behind his back, debating how to ask his next question.

Michael watched him thoughtfully. "You want to know whether *Lizzybell* can stay with you forever," He said, and took another sip of the drink.

Mr. Darcy nodded. "You can read my mind, too?"

Michael finished the last of the whisky and handed the empty flask back to Darcy. "I was not born yesterday. Why would you bring your best whisky if you were not hoping to bribe me for information or favor?"

"Well then, can she stay?"

"One small flask cannot make me drunk," Michael said.

"You are welcome to come back to my study after this. I have dozen of excellent bottles."

Michael laughed. "I like you, young man. You know what you want."

"So then, are you willing to allow Elizabeth to stay?"

"Unfortunately, I cannot make that decision. It is up to *Zenobie*."

"But you have known lost angels to fail to return to Heaven before, in your many years as Lost Angel Commissioner, have you not?"

"I am not allowed to discuss specific cases."

"Ah, so *there* have been cases of lost angels staying on Earth forever!"

"I did not tell you that. You came to your own conclusion." Michael turned to look at Elizabeth, then continued, "But *Zenobie* is soft-hearted. He is most unlike ordinary men. Indeed, he loves a romantic story."

"So he will allow it, if Elizabeth and I love each other deeply and desire to be together most fervently?"

Michael called out to Elizabeth that he had to leave. Then he bid his goodbye to Darcy by repeating, "I did not tell you such a thing. You drew your own conclusions."

Darcy's heart surged. There *was* a chance for them to have an eternity together!

As they flew back to Darcy House, Mr. Darcy could see that Elizabeth was very tired. He did not share the good news yet. Instead, they retired for the night, sleeping peacefully in each other's arms.

***

The journey back to Longbourn consisted of the Matlocks, the Bennets, the Gardiners, the Darcys and Mr. Bingley. Before the party set off for the journey, Mr. Darcy made everyone aware of the sleeping draft incident and his decision to cut off any connection he might have with Miss Bingley. Mr. Bingley, of course, was devastated. Everyone else was horrified at the tale of her machinations, and no one seemed to feel any great pang at the loss of her acquaintance.

While the Gardiners and Bennets settled back in at Longbourn for the wedding preparations, the rest of the party stayed at Netherfield.

It was agreed between Elizabeth and Mr. Darcy that, near midnight, she would fly to his bedchamber in Netherfield, summon Michael, and then bring Mr. Darcy with her to Meryton's graveyard.

They had quietly solicited the help of Colonel Fitzwilliam to intercept Miss de Bourgh and Mrs. Collins, by telling him that Mr. Collins seemed to have lost his mind after the accident in Rosings and had threatened to stop the wedding by harming Miss de Bourgh.

It was a dark, silent night when Elizabeth and Mr. Darcy reached the graveyard. The air was muggy and oppressive. Michael lagged behind and watched the proceedings from afar, to avoid the notice of any demon who might be present.

Suddenly an eerie sound echoed. "Come, *Lizzybell*! Bring Mr. Darcy into the mausoleum." It was *Corcifa*, speaking with the voice of Mr. Collins.

Mr. Darcy and Elizabeth looked at each other, then darted a glance towards Michael, but he was no longer visible. Hand in hand, the lovers took a deep breath and walked towards the mausoleum which held the body of the long-ago knight who had founded Meryton.

When they entered, braced for darkness, they were instead blinded by an abundance of candlelight. Hundreds of orange candles were burning, and flowers in all hues of orange adorned the mausoleum's interior.

Dressed in a silk wedding dress in similar colour with a long train, Miss Bingley stood close to Mr. Collins, wearing a smug smile. The dress was elegant, with intricate patterns embroidered onto it, but due to its similarity in colour to the flowers and the candles, the evil bride looked inconspicuous, except for her hat and her lips: she sported a high turban decorated with long, curvy black feathers, and her lips were, shockingly, painted in black.

Mr. Darcy flinched and Elizabeth gasped upon seeing Miss Bingley's bridal appearance. At her side, Mr. Collins was dressed normally, as a clergyman. He, too, wore a smug smile.

"I see that you have not worn your best clothes, Mr. Darcy." Mr. Collins shook his head in censure. "You should be ashamed of yourself, for your lovely bride has been waiting for you for many years. She has spent endless hours preparing herself for today's wedding – not to mention the wedding night."

He inclined his head. Following his gaze, Mr. Darcy and Elizabeth noticed for the first time that the top of the Meryton knight's tomb was covered with layers upon layers of orange silk sheets, with orange-hued petals scattered over them.

She expects me to have sexual congress with her atop a tomb, with a demon as witness? Mr. Darcy uttered silently to Elizabeth, disgusted and appalled.

She has truly taken leave of her senses, Elizabeth replied.

"No, no. Do not engage in mind talk with your ward, *Lizzybell*," Mr. Collins chastised. "How rude that is, when you know that Miss Bingley and I cannot hear you when you do so. Come, Mr. Darcy. It is time for the ceremony." He beckoned, and Mr. Darcy was shocked to feel his feet move forward as if they had a mind of their own.

Elizabeth looked at her ward anxiously, biting her lips, determined to wait as she had been instructed to do by Michael, the night before.

"Now take the left hand of your lovely bride," Mr. Collins ordered.

When Miss Bingley extended her hand to him, Mr. Darcy could see that her fingernails were painted black and orange, and that she bore a large, artistic 'C' depicted in orange on her palm.

Drawing in a deep breath, Mr. Darcy pulled his waistcoat, then put his right hand on her left and squeezed it hard.

"Aiee!" Miss Bingley screamed in agony, and doubled over, grabbing her left palm with her right hand.

As Mr. Darcy jumped back to where Elizabeth stood waiting, she chanted her angelic verse quickly and spread her wings.

"You hurt my protégé!" Mr. Collins exclaimed, and his countenance turned furious. "I will crush you, low-level angel!" He tore off his clothes, showing a chest covered in green hair. Then, to the astonishment of the angelic couple, a green ring appeared on his head, just above his eyebrows.

With a flick of his hands, he blew Mr. Darcy and Elizabeth off their feet, and they hit the wall with punishing force. Mr. Darcy hurt his head and nearly lost consciousness, while Elizabeth's shoulders were injured.

Then Mr. Collins turned his palm and drew them back to himself. Mr. Darcy was helpless, dragged along the floor towards the demon. He tried to break the pull by turning towards Elizabeth. She scrambled in an effort to catch hold of Darcy's hand, but in vain.

Mr. Darcy had been pulled very close to the ringed man's feet by the time Elizabeth finally managed to stand up and take a wooden dagger from her boot. She lunged towards Mr. Collins, aiming at his heart, but the demon was fast, turning his body aside immediately.

As a result, she missed him and fell forward, accidentally slashing Miss Bingley, who was sitting nearby, still in pain from her encounter with Mr. Darcy.

"Bloody...! Collins, kill her..." Miss Bingley cried. "What do I pay you for? Oh... blood on my arm." She held her injured limb, wailing.

"Shut up," Mr. Collins retorted. "What do you think I am trying to do?" Leaning forward, he tried to disarm Elizabeth. She flicked her hand and pushed Miss Bingley towards him instead, then hurriedly flew behind him.

Miss Bingley tried to cling to him, but Mr. Collins shook her off, turned his head, and breathed out a gust of green ice towards Elizabeth. With her wings beating at high speed,

Lizzybell arced over the devil's freezing flame, swooped down at him and plunged her wooden dagger into his heart.

"No!" Miss Bingley screamed as the demon writhed and howled. "No! You cannot die. You must still make Mr. Darcy marry me!"

Mr. Darcy and Elizabeth watched in wary exultation as *Corcifa* fell back to lean on the tomb. Mr. Darcy ran to his angel's side but, before they could celebrate, Mr. Collins gave a loud roar. Pulling himself up straight, he jerked the wooden dagger out of his body and threw it at the wall.

"Idiotic Michael," Mr. Collins yelled. "I am not the *Corcifa* of seven years ago. A tiny dagger dipped in pig's blood cannot hurt me anymore."

To Darcy's and Elizabeth's utter surprise, the hole in the demon's heart sealed, and a green furry ball came out from his back.

Michael appeared before them, flustered by this turn of events. "Damnation! I shall check to see whether he has other weaknesses." With that, he drew his black book out of his sleeve and flicked through it quickly.

"Ha!" *Corcifa* turned his hands and again drew the shocked couple towards him. "Take your time, Michael. Take your time, while I eat your pretty angel alive!" He bared his teeth, which had now turned a sickening green.

"Wrap around me!" Elizabeth yelled. Mr. Darcy did as he was told, encircling her neck with his arms and her hips with his legs, and thus avoided being dragged towards the demon, while Elizabeth made a Herculean effort to stand firm.

Seeing that his pull was ineffective, Mr. Collins blew icy green fire at them again. Elizabeth flew up, with Darcy still tightly wrapped around her. Then she pushed her hand into the pocket of Darcy's coat and took out a black pine cone, wrapped in cloth and tied with a red ribbon. She wrapped the ribbon around her hand and threw the cone at Mr. Collins.

He ducked, while he continued to breathe ice towards them.

"Michael, search faster!" Mr. Darcy yelled anxiously as Elizabeth continued to throw the cone at the demon, drawing it back by its ribbon each time it missed, then throwing it again.

"I know, I know." Michael flipped and flipped as he cast an anxious glance at the menacing demon.

Suddenly, the tip of Elizabeth's right wing was struck by the green ice. With a groan of pain, she dropped to the ground.

"Elizabeth!" Darcy cried anxiously, as Michael called, "*Lizzybell!*"

She contorted in pain as *Corcifa* approached them. When he extended his hawk-like hand to drag Darcy off his angel, Elizabeth wrapped her left hand around Darcy's waist, lunged up from the ground, and plunged the pine cone directly into the demon's heart.

With a shriek, Collins staggered off, as Elizabeth disentangled the ribbon from her wrist.

"Pull out that stupid cone and kill the country chit!" Miss Bingley yelled. "I want to get married and be Mrs. Darcy *now*."

Corcifa put his hand on the ribbon and tried to draw the black cone out, but he could not. His eyes widened in alarm as he saw green fluid flowing from his heart wound.

"You cannot die!" Miss Bingley hissed. "*Corcifa*, you promised me a lifetime of wealth and importance as Mrs. Darcy! You swore it would be so!" But even as she spoke, the furry beast left the body of Collins, with the cone still stuck in his chest, and disappeared into thin air.

"I found it!" Michael cried, having belatedly found the information he sought. "A black female pine cone dipped in the fluid of a virgin male can kill him, and a pine needle soaked in the same fluid can injure his protégé."

He looked at them and blinked. "Mr. Darcy, what are you doing?"

Elizabeth drew a deep breath and said patiently, "I know. I asked the *petna*, this afternoon, and prepared the cone and the pine needle together with my nephew Thomas Gardiner. Fitzwilliam touched Miss Bingley's palm with the pine needle just now. He is piercing her hand with it now. I wanted something more to reply on, in case you were not correct about the pig blood."

Across the mausoleum, Miss Bingley began to contort in pain as Mr. Darcy retreated, his mission accomplished. Her body rolled on the floor a few times until, with a last jerky movement, she lay motionless beside the body of Mr. Collins.

"Are they alive?" Elizabeth asked uneasily.

Michael approached them to check. He found that Mr. Collins was dead but Miss Bingley was still alive. The skin of her left hand and arm was covered by an array of ugly scars. The fabric of the orange wedding dress seemed to have dissolved into the skin itself, coloring the scars in livid hues of orange and black.

CHAPTER FORTEEN

As Michael returned to report to Elizabeth and Mr. Darcy about the state of their enemies, he saw that the low-level angel was sitting on the cold stone floor, also in pain.

"Michael, Elizabeth is hurt. Can you help her?" Mr. Darcy asked anxiously.

Michael nodded. "That I am most assuredly allowed to do…but I think she would prefer your aid. You may reward your angel by kissing her better."

"Can I really?" Mr. Darcy asked, unsure whether this was an angelic rule or whether Michael was jesting with him.

"Certainly. *Lizzybell* was magnificent in protecting you, and so she deserves to be rewarded by her ward. I shall take Miss Bingley back to Netherfield, dispose of Collins's body, and check on the well-being of Miss de Bourgh."

Mr. Darcy was glad of Michael's help. He much preferred to take care of his beloved, at that moment. Gingerly, Darcy settled by her side, wrapped his arm around Elizabeth's waist, kissed her injured shoulder and drew the burned wing forward so that he could kiss the darkened feathers.

Elizabeth moaned. Mr. Darcy was unsure whether she had experienced agony or ecstasy from his kiss, but he could see that the black colour had turned slightly lighter, from black to grey. Heartened, he continued to trace a line of kisses over the burnt feathers, making Elizabeth moan and squirm for several long minutes. Her hands instinctively smoothed over his injured head and his back, rubbing and kneading there.

"Can you fly now?" he asked, with a smile and a heated stare of arousal, when the feathers had at last returned to white. "Shall we adjourn to my bedchamber?"

"Yes, please," she said, sounding quite recovered. "That is an excellent plan." Elizabeth stood up, closed her eyes and concentrated on his room.

"Wait! What about me?" Mr. Darcy chased out of the mausoleum as he saw her take off to the sky without him.

Then the wind shifted, and his angel returned. With an arch of her eyebrows and a saucy smile, she landed gracefully before him. He returned the smile, approached her and kissed her passionately on the mouth before wrapping his hands around her neck and his legs around her hips. He moved his body, rubbing against her provocatively, and she shivered, locking her hands around her waist.

"It is good to drive away the demon," she whispered in his ear.

"I am glad you are my angel," he replied, and kissed her earlobe.

Elizabeth closed her eyes, concentrated, and took them up into the sky again.

"Is it possible to make love in the sky?" Mr. Darcy asked suddenly, as his arousal grew stronger.

Elizabeth's heart nearly stopped at the outrageous inquiry, and they lost altitude abruptly. "Do not say another *word* until we reach your bed," she entreated.

He kept his mouth shut but continued to kiss her neck and shoulders.

Shaking her head at her rebellious ward, she drew in a deep breath and flew them precariously to his room. When they reached the destination, she pushed him on the bed, turned him face-down, and smacked his bottom smartly.

"Were you trying to crash us?" She demanded.

"Ouch!" he yelled in pain and buried his face in the coverlet.

"Oh!" Elizabeth stopped immediately, "Did my angelic strength hurt you?"

But when she tried to turn him over to check on him, he rolled over and pushed her onto the bed, face-down, instead. "Now it is my turn to give you a good smack," he said with a laugh. Then he pulled her dress and shift up, exposing her pert bottom to his gaze. He positioned his hand over the flesh, and she held her breath.

When he touched her smooth skin, however, he did not have the heart to smack her, after all that she had done to protect him. Instead, he rubbed both hands in caressing circles on her bottom's creamy cheeks, massaging them.

From fearful anticipation, Elizabeth melted into an ecstatic moan. Then she began to pant as Darcy lowered his mouth to kiss and lick the curved flesh of her bottom. When he parted her thighs and slid his hot tongue along her folds from behind, she startled herself by coming in an instant. Trembling, shivering, she felt the blood riot in her veins as she jerked and convulsed, utterly transported.

Mesmerised by her peak, he stripped off his trousers immediately and pressed his huge shaft into her from behind in a single mighty thrust, aided by the way that her orgasmic juices had moistened her hot entrance, as if begging for his invasion.

She screamed in ecstasy, while he buried his face in her wings. His hands slid under her to rub her breasts and tweak her impudent nipples. Inspired, he jerked forward farther, intent on penetrating deeply enough to touch her very core. His tip vibrated, his rod creating friction against every inch of her inner muscles, branding her sleek inner skin. She was stretched as he had never stretched her before, filled in every direction.

He pulled back swiftly, nearly to her entrance, then pushed back in, irresistible as he claimed her body. She moaned and yelped as she felt him pounding and thrusting into her again and again, on and on.

Her nipples were puckered hard as he palmed and squeezed her breasts. His rampant manhood glided over her folds and prodded her apex, stroking her to a fever pitch. And all the while, the sensitive flesh of her bottom was grazed and titillated by his coarse bush and hot, heavy scrotum.

Every time his stout rod buried itself deeply inside her, her soft butt cheeks felt as if they were being spanked. Her tender bottom and all of the muscles hidden inside her core burned for almost half an hour under his lusty ministrations, and the sensations tipped her over the edge three more times. Or was it longer and did she enjoy more orgasms? She realised, dazed, that she had lost count. She only knew that her Mr. Darcy was an insatiable man. His pounding, thrusting and squeezing of her body did not stop until, sobbing for breath, he took her to the summit yet again.

Oh what a night to win over the demon and make love so passionately! That was her last thought before she slipped into a sated slumber, with her dearest love still buried deep within her.

***

The next morning, the Darcys and the Matlocks found that they had the house to themselves. Mr. Bingley left a very private letter to Darcy, explaining that his sister had appeared in the early hours at Netherfield, dressed in a blood-stained wedding dress, injured and delusional. She claimed that she was Mr. Darcy's bride, and repeatedly called for Mr. Collins to begin the ceremony.

Mr. Bingley was at a loss to imagine how she had come to be in such a state. He summoned a doctor to tend to her, and later decided to take her back to London to Hurst's townhouse, where she would receive better care. He also admitted not wanting to disturb Darcy's preparation for the happy event, but he promised to return in time for Darcy's wedding.

Mr. Darcy was relieved to know that the delusional, tainted woman had been removed from the proximity of his sister and betrothal, and his mood brightened further when he found that Colonel Fitzwilliam had been successful in retrieving his cousin Anne. She appeared unharmed, though still weak from fever and travel. Mrs. Collins, not privy to the scheme of the demon, was under the impression that they were travelling back to Hertfordshire to attend Elizabeth's wedding.

However the neighbourhood was in an uproar, as the news of Mr. Collins' demise reached them. His body had been discovered in Meryton's graveyard, with no apparent external wounds. An expensive-looking turban made of fine fabric and decorated with long, curved, black feathers was found lying beside him.

The Lucas family was inconsolable, to have their daughter left a widow at such a young age and without any monetary inheritance left to her. While the Bennet family was shocked by the death of Mr. Collins, Mrs. Bennet could not help but feel relieved that the entailment was finally broken. The first-born son of any of her daughters would now inherit the Longbourn estate.

On a beautiful and sunny April day, Miss Elizabeth Bennet became Mrs. Fitzwilliam Darcy of Pemberley, in a happy and moving ceremony. The wedding reception at Netherfield Park was as grand and sumptuous as it was joyous.

Mr. Darcy could not take his eyes off his bride during the entire morning, for she was radiant, witty and elegant. He did not mind the jests of his relatives and friends, saying he was besotted and tongue-tied. He was busy memorising every detail of his wonderful wife and the happiest day of his life, and he had no attention to spare for engaging in casual pleasantries. He did not release his wife's hand for more than a few minutes after they were declared husband and wife.

When he left for London, finally alone with his bride, he enjoyed sharing sweet conversation, tender caresses and frequent kisses with his beloved. By the time they reached Darcy House, he could not wait for the night, but hurried his wife to their bedchamber after the lightest of refreshments.

"What is the rush, my dear?" Elizabeth raised her eyebrows as she saw her husband shut the door firmly. "I was hoping to have a discussion with our housekeeper, Mrs. Waterston, about..."

Mr. Darcy lowered his head and nipped her lips, not allowing her to finish the sentence. As he suckled the soft, wet flesh, his hands moved to rub her shapely bottom. His skin felt the fabric of the wedding dress and traced the wildflower pattern sewn on it. The contrast of the uneven texture of the dress and the firm, smooth muscles of her bottom sent shivers through his body. His arousal strained within his trousers, and his body heated up.

He moved closer to the source of pleasure, imprinting her soft valleys and hills with his hard body. As their kiss became deeper, their hands grew more frantic about displacing each other's clothes. But once they were stripped down to their naked glory, they stepped back from each other, breathing heavily, each devouring the other's form with hungry eyes.

As she moved to recline on the bed, he followed eagerly and began their first journey of exploration as husband and wife. The afternoon sun spilled into the room. For the first time, they did not have to conceal their union or rush their pleasures, for they were loving each other with the sanction of their families and society, not as stolen moments in the dead of the night.

Their kisses were tender, their caresses were slow and sweet. When Mr. Darcy finally thrust into her, after almost an hour of exploration, joining their bodies, Elizabeth felt a heart-warming joy burst within her. He was hers. This wonderful, handsome, intelligent man was hers.

Every inch of this incredible man was uniting with her, body and soul. His mouth breathed into hers, his chest rubbed against hers, his hands grabbed hers, and his glorious manhood fitted perfectly within her. There was no room at all for worries about the future, or even the present. Nothing separated her from him. They were one soul.

Soon, she felt him moving, in and out, slowly, allowing her to enjoy the glissade, the heat and friction created by his body. He made a bold advance, then beat a clever retreat, again and again, still moving at a snail's pace.

She did nothing to hurry him. Her hands enjoyed a journey of their own, smoothing over his strong, muscled back, from his shoulders down to the base of his spine.

When she slid her fingers along the clenched cheeks of his buttocks, she seemed to have touched a sensitive spot in his soul. His whole body shuddered for a second, and then he picked up the pace, pounding into her with maddening speed.

His huge, hot rod impaled her wet core, never faltering. She arched her body upward, meeting him thrust for thrust, until they both reached their peaks, burst into flame and screaming out in ecstasy.

The shivering and shimmering went on and on, his seed flooding her womb. Then an unearthly peace filled them, soothing them as their breathing finally resumed.

"I love you, Fitzwilliam," she proclaimed in a hoarse voice. "Forever."

He wiped the tiny beads of perspiration from her forehead and replied, "Forever, Elizabeth. I love you."

Mr. and Mrs. Darcy did not make an appearance downstairs until very late the next afternoon. After that, they spent a few days alone in London, without visitors, enjoying each other's company and love-making before heading back to Pemberley, to fulfill Darcy's happy ambition of showing his bride their home.

***

It was there, a week after Elizabeth and Mr. Darcy settled happily at Pemberley, that bad news arrived unexpectedly by express, in the dead of the night.

"What is it, my dear?" Mr. Darcy hastened to enfold his trembling wife, urging her to sit down. "What did the express say?"

"It is the most dreadful news. It is Lydia!" Elizabeth sat down, fighting for breath, trying to hold back her tears and her anger. "She has eloped – abandoned all her family and friends – and has thrown herself into the power of Mr. Wickham!"

"That damnable scoundrel!" Mr. Darcy swore, and started to pace. "How did it happen? What has been done?"

"Jane writes that Lydia left Longbourn on Sunday night. They did not discover that she was missing until Monday morning. She says that Lydia left a letter, saying that they were travelling directly to Gretna Green, and that Papa has left to attempt to trace them immediately. But there is no further news yet. She has written to Uncle Gardiner, as well, to beg for his assistance. Oh, how could Lydia be so stupid? It is all my fault." Elizabeth was crying in earnest now.

"It is not your fault." Mr. Darcy knelt in front of her, wrapped his arms around her shoulders and hugged her tight. "Indeed, I fear that it is my fault. I should have told the neighbourhood of the scoundrel."

"But I knew who he was. Had his character been known, this could not have happened. Now, it is all, all too late."

"Do not distress yourself any more than you can help, my dear," he said. "I shall go to London tomorrow, find the rake, and force him to marry Lydia."

"But nothing can be done! He is a tempting angel. No amount of money or connection can induce him to marry her."

"What?" He recoiled in shock. "Wickham is a tempting angel?"

"Yes, he confessed it to me in Hertfordshire. His angelic name is *PickyWickly*. He got Michael drunk, and the Lost Angel Commissioner told him about the other angels he was tracking. That is how Mr. Wickham learned that I am a guardian angel. He said that his duty is to tempt humans to their downfall."

Mr. Darcy sat heavily on his heels, lost for words. Then a thought came to him. "What if you call for Michael and I give him the best whisky? He may reveal some secrets that we can use to work on Wickham."

Elizabeth raised her teary eyes, hope dawning, and nodded eagerly.

"Let me begin by asking Wharton to prepare for the journey to London anyway," he said.

"I shall go with you. I shall ask my maid, Sarah, as well," she said, and he agreed.

When they had briefly instructed Wharton and Sarah, the unhappy couple went back to their bedchamber, where Elizabeth took out the *petna* and requested Michael's appearance. But after writing his name and calling out for him a dozen times, the high-level angel still did not appear.

Elizabeth threw the quill down onto the table, trembling with frustration.

"Come, Elizabeth. He may simply be busy at the moment." He took her to lie down. "Let us get some rest while we can. We will need our strength, tomorrow."

The household at Pemberley was awakened very early, the next day, to yet another express. This time it was addressed to the master.

"Oh my God!" Mr. Darcy said, after reading the letter.

"Another bad tiding?" Elizabeth asked in a trembling voice.

He signaled for his wife to follow him to the study. "It is from Richard. He says that Anne left Matlock House with her companion yesterday morning, and did not return. He fears that she has gone to find Wickham!"

"How can that be possible? Does she know of Lydia's demise?" she asked, frowning as she tried to imagine a link between the incidents.

Mr. Darcy was parchment pale. "No. After questioning the servant that serves as her maid, Lady Matlock believes that Anne may be with child." Shakily, he poured himself a glass of whisky.

"What? Surely that cannot be!"

"They searched Anne's room thoroughly, and found that Mrs. Jenkinson, her companion, had sent a letter to her, a day earlier, saying that she had received intelligence about Wickham. He has returned to Derbyshire. Richard believes that Anne's child must be Wickham's, and that she left with Mrs. Jenkinson to come here. He begs for my assistance."

"That *PickyWickly*! He has been most busy doing his duty, tempting every woman crossing his path." She stood up and paced. "Did Miss de Bourgh know him for very long?"

"Yes, I fear she did. Father brought him along occasionally when we visited Rosings. But what I do not understand is how he could seduce her and your sister both, in such a short span of time."

"I wonder at it, as well. Wickham's stay in Hertfordshire was of short duration. He must have left after our encounter in the woods. Lydia had only seen him three times, and always in the company of others, unless..." She stopped, her eyes widening.

"Unless what?"

"Unless she met with him during her walks around Hunsford."

"The rake must have left Meryton after the Netherfield ball and gone to Kent to use his charms on Anne. Then he met up with Miss Lydia and seduced her." He scowled. "But she only went outdoors for a short while, when you had fainted, an hour at the most."

"I have never known Lydia to enjoy walking for an hour. How remiss of me!" She went to pour herself a measure of wine and gulped it down in a single mouthful.

"Mmm, her appearance did look rather dishevelled when she came in."

"For certain! She said she liked it in Hunsford. And she said it with a smug countenance. And she was quite agitated when she was told that she must leave it." She put the glass down roughly. "So what are we to do?"

"If Wickham is in Derbyshire, I shall find him." He took her hand and kissed her forehead. "I shall talk to Wharton and have him send out some men to Lambton and other likely possible places. Did you want to go back to rest some more? You slept fitfully last night."

"No." She shook her head vehemently. "I shall ask for Michael again. If he does not make an appearance, I shall ask the *petna* about tempting angels. After all, *PickyWickly* is only the lowest kind of angel. There must be something that I can do, to make him pay for trifling with my sister and your cousin."

***

Late in the afternoon, Mr. Darcy came into the bedchamber where Elizabeth was resting.

"Elizabeth, Wharton has spotted Wickham in a tavern in Rushcliffe, a little town about five miles north of Pemberley and Lambton."

She bolted up from the bed. "Are we going to wait for Colonel Fitzwilliam?"

Mr. Darcy shook his head. "Wharton says Wickham was in the tavern alone. He paid a little lad to watch over the scoundrel while he came back to report to me. We may lose his trail if we wait."

"Then I shall come with you," she said, and got ready rapidly.

A few minutes into their journey, the skies opened up and heavy rain fell. He looked out of the carriage window with concern. The road to Rushcliffe was steep and narrow, as it zigzagged up and down the hill, with the rock face on one side and a deep valley descending on the other. With mud and slippery rock, the carriage journey had quickly become both uncomfortable and dangerous.

He turned to his wife, trying to distract her mind from her worries. "So Michael did not respond?"

"No. It was most vexing."

"And what did you find out from the *petna* about tempting angels?"

"It was nearly useless, as well. It just told me what their duties were – those which *PickyWickly* had told me already. It said I had no business in delving into that particular detail concerning other angels! I hate that *Himins* has such strict rules on certain things while ..."

Crack!

The sound of something breaking was followed by a sudden lurch of the carriage.

"Hold tight!" Mr. Darcy wrapped one hand around Elizabeth's waist while he used the other to hold onto the wooden frame of the window. Glancing out, he saw that stones were tumbling down the rocky slope, startling the horses, and forcing the carriage to slide off the road. The left-side wheels crackled ominously as the carriage skidded farther towards the edge.

Suddenly the carriage door sprang open, and Mr. Darcy and Elizabeth tumbled out of it. He tried to hold onto his wife, but his head struck a rock, and he lost consciousness.

Before Elizabeth could chant the angelic verse and spread her wings to save them, lightning flashed. She jumped instinctively away from the light, becoming separated from her husband. When she turned back, she could only watch with frightened eyes as a purple streak of light hit him.

"NO!" she screamed in anguish, but the scene before her did not change: her husband was lying on the rocky slope, motionless.

CHAPTER FIFTEEN

"Wake up! Oh, please, wake up!"

"Darcy, can you hear me?"

Mr. Darcy opened his eyes and saw the anxious faces of Georgiana and Colonel Fitzwilliam hovering over him. He tried to turn his head, but the movement proved too painful.

"What happened?" he asked, but his voice came out as a whisper; his throat was parched, and his lips would hardly open.

"Your carriage slid off the road due to a rock slide. Wharton and the footmen were knocked unconscious for nearly half an hour. When they came around, they found you and then went to find help. I had arrived at Pemberley by then, so we took you back," his cousin said.

"Where is Elizabeth?" Darcy tried to rise from the bed but his shoulders hurt as well. "Is she all right?"

Georgiana burst into tears at this juncture.

"What is wrong? Why are you crying, Georgiana? Is Elizabeth…" He asked frantically, trying to get himself up and check on his wife. "Is she injured?"

"Do not move, Darcy. You will only hurt yourself," Colonel Fitzwilliam said. He looked down at Darcy's worried face and decided to be truthful. "Mrs. Darcy is missing."

"Missing? How can that be? I was holding her when the accident occurred. Perhaps she, too, went to seek aid for me. What has been done to locate her?"

"Wharton and the others did not see Mrs. Darcy with you when they found you. They thought she might have been thrown farther down the slope. While we brought you back, I had several men search the area. They found nothing. It is dark now. The rain has not yet stopped. I had to postpone the search. It is too dangerous for them to continue, and there is too great a chance that they would miss seeing something important. We will begin again, at first light."

Mr. Darcy was appalled. "But we cannot leave her to lie unprotected on the slope overnight. With the heavy rains, she could be seriously injured and die," he protested, and struggled again to sit up.

"Cousin, you must be prepared. She may have already died, if she was thrown down the valley."

"No! We have been together for such a short time. She cannot leave me..." Mr. Darcy cried out.

Suddenly all strength left him. He slumped back onto the bed and closed his eyes, remembering. *She was required to return to Heaven when the time came. But did Michael not say that she could stay here, if she and I both wanted it ardently enough? How could they knock me unconscious and not allow me to express my wish? Did Elizabeth not want to stay with me fervently? I refuse to believe it. She seemed so happy with me, every day.*

Tears ran down his face. "Do not leave me, my angel. How can you protect me when you are gone? Did you not love me enough? Did you go back to Heaven willingly? Why?"

"Brother, what are you talking about? Please, wake up." Georgiana cried. She had never seen him in such wild despair.

"I think it is the fever, Georgiana," Colonel Fitzwilliam said. "I shall ask the doctor to tend to him again. Tomorrow, as soon as day breaks, be assured that I shall resume the search for

Mrs. Darcy. And I must go to Rushcliffe, as well, to check on the whereabouts of Anne." Georgiana nodded, tears streaming down her face.

***

As to Elizabeth, when the lightning struck her husband, she had seen with wide and frightened eyes that he was hurt. She had not been quick enough to protect him. As she began to rush to him, another lightning flashed, and Michael appeared directly in front of her, blocking her path.

"He is hurt, Michael!"

"It is time."

"Time?"

"Yes, time for you to return to *Himins*."

"No!" Elizabeth shook her head fiercely. "My husband is injured. I must stay with him and find help."

"If your concern is his wellbeing, you can guard him better from *Himins*."

"I saved him from the clutches of *Corcifa* on Earth. I can guard him well here, too."

Michael looked at her soberly. "If you do not go now, there may not be another chance to return."

"But I love him. How can I leave him, especially now, when he is hurt? We did not even say goodbye. He would be heartbroken if he wakes and finds me gone, forever," she said in a trembling voice.

"He knew of that possibility when he married you."

"It will not make it hurt any less. I am hurting now. I shall be heartbroken if I cannot see him anymore." Tears rushed down her face.

"Ah, but you will still be able to see him from *Himins*. You are his guardian angel. You simply will not be able to talk to him."

"No. I am still not going. I hate *Himins*. I hate you. I hate *PickyWickly*. I hate *Zenobie*. I hate his wife. I hate his twin…"

Another voice interrupted her tirade. "Low-level angel," it said sternly, "you are very disrespectful!"

Elizabeth looked towards the source of the voice, then wiped the tears from her eyes, to make sure she was seeing clearly. Still startled, she closed them and opened them again. But it was true: she was in a garden filled with golden flowers and lush green shrubbery. A man with short curly blond hair, wearing a golden robe, was seated on a marble chair. He looked quite young, close to Darcy's age. He looked up from the book he had been reading and scowled at her.

Then she looked to his left, and saw Mr. Wickham there. "You!" she hissed.

"Ah, *Lizzybell*." He gave her a deep bow. "We meet again."

She ignored him and looked again for her husband. Left and right, she scanned, but he was no longer there.

At her side, Michael gave a slight nod downward, towards their feet. Following his gaze, she saw Mr. Darcy, through a gap in the cloud under their feet, lying motionless on his bed.

"No!" Tears welled in her eyes again. "I do not want to be here. I want to go back."

"What do you have against *Himins*?" asked the man in the golden robe, putting down his book. "Michael, why is it that both of these two lost angels wish to stay on Earth?"

Michael looked startled. "*PickyWickly* does not want to stay here either?"

Mr. Wickham answered for himself. "After a few days here I realise I enjoy my duty on Earth more. I had just found a rich woman to marry, and I want the taste of a life of luxury again."

"Scoundrel!" Elizabeth cried. "What have you done to Miss de Bourgh and Lydia?"

"Anne is carrying my child, and we are to marry in Rushcliffe in two days time," he said proudly. "I am certain that I can get rid of Lady Catherine soon afterwards, since she has been sick for the past few weeks. After Anne inherits Rosings, she will soon rest in peace, from exhaustion from my ardent love-making or from some ailment. She is a frail thing, you know. Then, with her money at my disposal, I can set myself up in London in style. As for your sister, she is in London already. I think she will enjoy her stay there."

"She is not travelling with you?"

"As you can see, I cannot be in two places at once." Wickham shrugged and continued. "After she most willingly permitted me to capture her virtue in Kent, I have kept in touch with her. When she expressed a wish to marry me, I sent a carriage for her to join me in London. My good friend Mrs. Younge will take good care of her for the time being, while I am dealing with Anne."

"Mrs. Younge!" Elizabeth hissed. "That horrible governess of Georgiana? What do you intend to do to my sister?"

"I have not made up my mind yet. It all depends upon you. But Mrs. Younge does know of establishments that cater to a man's every need. If you make trouble for me, I may have Mrs. Younge introduce your sister to some of her friends."

"I shall kill you!" Elizabeth cried out, and ran forward to strike the scoundrel.

"No brawling here," *Zenobie* said firmly. With a flick of his hand, he stopped Elizabeth's advance, freezing her on the spot. "Now, *PickyWickly*, I ask you one more time to stay in *Himins*, where you can enjoy your life here and perform your tempting duty by appearing in people's mind, too. Is that not a powerful situation to savour?"

"I mean no offense to *Himins*, Mr. *Zenobie*, but I think I would rather do more tempting on Earth. I am used to being down there. The angels here do not seem to be very interested in a lower-level angel like myself, and the wine here – if you will pardon me for saying so – is awful. On Earth, I shall have real action, rather than engaging only in mind games."

Zenobie nodded his head. "You did well, *PickyWickly*, in tempting humans to commit sin so far. I think you deserve a promotion. As a level-six angel, you will get more notice from the higher-level female angels. Are you absolutely certain? You truly do not want to stay here?"

"You cannot promote him!" Elizabeth raised her voice and glared at *Zenobie*. "In fact, he should be punished."

Zenobie stood up. Nearly twice the height of Elizabeth, he towered over her. Folding his arms, he pressed his lips thin. "He is only doing his duty. Why should I punish him? It is you who has been most disrespectful. You expressed a dislike of both *Himins* and myself. And now you seek to interfere with my authority. I think that *you* are the one who should be punished."

"Why should I be? I am just doing my duty." Elizabeth tilted her defiantly and looked at the fearsome deity with a determined expression "My ward wishes me to stay with him forever, and that is what I want to do, and what I should do. *PickyWickly* is trifling with my ward's cousin, Anne, and my earthly sister, Lydia. This threatens the well-being of Mr. Darcy's mind. It is my responsibility to prevent *PickyWickly* from so doing. If you promote and endorse his actions, you are in fact acting unfairly, favouring his work while undermining mine."

"She is right," said a female voice. "You cannot favour one angel's work against another's." Every one turned, on hearing the young woman.

"*Zara*! You wish to interfere with your father's work, too?" *Zenobie* said to the young woman, who had dark, curly hair, a handsome face and expressive eyes. She looked about twenty, too old to be *Zenobie*'s daughter.

Elizabeth was happy that someone agreed with her. Taking heart, she pushed on. "And he was a tempting angel only. Why is it that you allow him to plan the murders of Lady Catherine and Miss de Bourgh?"

The dark-haired young woman laughed in delight. "Well, Father, I see that you are losing your argument with a level-six angel," the young woman said, and moved to take Elizabeth's hand, drawing her from the frozen spot effectively. "*Lizzybell*, I am delighted to meet you at last. I am *Zarala*, *Zenobie*'s daughter. But I was Mrs. Bennet's daughter when I was on Earth."

"What?" Elizabeth felt utterly bewildered. She had never thought about the fate of her... predecessor.

"Come and sit. I want to chat with you while Father deals with *PickyWickly*," *Zarala* said, and frowned at the tempting angel.

So, she does not like Mr. Wickham, either, Elizabeth thought happily. *I have someone to champion my argument.* "I would rather stay to hear *Zenobie*'s decision, as it concerns my – I mean your – sister, Miss Bennet." Elizabeth was confused about what to call her new-found ally.

"You may call me *Zara*. I have only been known by the name of Lizzy for a week," *Zarala* said. "So, Father, be quick. What are you going to do with *PickyWickly*? I wish to chat with *Lizzybell* for a bit, afterwards."

"Sir, I should not be punished. I am only doing my job," Wickham said, looking at *Zarala* anxiously. He wished bitterly that he had not tried to win some favours from that woman, the other day. He had been drunk on *Himins*'s bad wine and had not known she was *Zenobie*'s daughter.

"You may return to Earth, *PickyWickly*. Just do not commit murder." *Zenobie* sat down again, looking pensive. He could never deny his daughter anything, and she seemed to like *Lizzybell*. "However, you do know that your angelic skills will diminish when you choose this path, do you not?"

"What do you mean? I did not know about that," Wickham said. "Should I reconsider and stay here?"

"Your body will gradually become more human," Michael explained. "For example, unlike your present state as a tempting angel, your ability to impregnate women will no longer be ten out of ten attempts."

"That I can live with," Wickham said. "I do not need a whole herd of bastards underfoot."

"He makes women be with child, every time?" Elizabeth said. Her hand covered her forehead. "Then Lydia is with child by him, now."

"That is a so-called 'trick of his trade'," *Zarala* said. "It is essential for a tempting angel. Unfortunately, our silly sister succumbed to his temptation. She must bear with – and bear – the result."

Mr. Wickham smiled with satisfaction and bowed to everyone. "In that case, I should like to go back on Earth now. My wealthy bride is waiting for me. Au revoir, *Lizzybell*."

"If that is your desire, then so be it." *Zenobie* shrugged, took out a quill, opened his book and struck Wickham's name from the angel register. As he did so, Wickham's body disappeared.

Zarala clapped her hands and hugged Michael. "Thank you for your help, Michael. I did not want the sleazy creature here."

Zenobie smiled at all three of them. "And I was only pretending to want him to stay."

"Oh, Father, you acted so convincingly that you fooled me, as well."

"Give me some credit, my dear. I know that he got drunk, the other day, and tried to force himself on you." *Zenobie* wrapped his arm around his daughter and gave her a kiss on the forehead. "Of course, you gave him what he deserved. That was why I allowed Michael not to tell him that his luck at avoiding retribution from angry parents, husbands and creditors on Earth will gradually run out as well, as he is no longer protected by his tempting-angel status."

"That is good to hear," Elizabeth said. "Then will you allow me to rejoin my husband on Earth too?"

"Are you absolutely certain that this is what you want?" Michael asked. "You will gradually lose your angelic skills, like flying, too."

"I do not mind about that." Elizabeth said, but then she thought of something else. Biting her lip, she asked, "If I am no longer Mr. Darcy's guardian angel, who will protect him?"

"Only people who have done good deeds have a guardian angel," *Zenobie* said, preparing to write something in his book. "Mr. Darcy was wicked when he demanded you sleep with him against your wishes. He will no longer have a guardian angel."

"But that is not true!" Elizabeth protested immediately. "You did not take me away then, immediately after Mr. Darcy made his 'wicked' demand. You effectively endorsed his action. You cannot go back and revoke your decision, weeks afterwards."

"Oh, you *are* one impertinent low-level angel!" *Zenobie* threw down his quill and threw up his hands.

"Father, you lose your argument again!" *Zarala* chuckled. "Do not worry, *Lizzybell*. Your husband is a good man. Father will assign him another guardian angel when you become truly human."

"Thank you, *Zarala*." Another thought struck her, and her eyes grew large. "Oh! When I truly become… Does that mean that I will be able to bear him a child, one day?" Elizabeth asked, brightening at the thought.

"Go and chat with *Zara* for a bit," *Zenobie* said. "Your wits are too quick for an old man like me. Michael, let us go for a drink. I need to fortify myself, after dealing with this low-level angel here."

CHAPTER SIXTEEN

"*Zara*, I am eager to talk to you too, but I am even more anxious to return to my husband's side," Elizabeth said as *Zarala* led her away through a gap in the shrubbery.

"Do not worry. Mr. Darcy will not be in grave danger. But he is indeed quite wicked, demanding you to do his bidding after he learned about your situation in Kent. So he must be punished."

"But I do not resent his demands. I am thrilled that he wants me all the time. I do not want him punished," Elizabeth said as they continued to walk along the winding path.

"I know. Ah! Here is my favourite place." *Zarala* stopped. In front of them was a little pond, with gently steamy water trickling down from a high rock face. Tall, sturdy trees shaded half of the pond, and chairs were scattered around.

"Come. Let me show you what his punishment will be." *Zarala* signaled for her to sit by her side as she took up one of the books, flipped through its pages, and showed Elizabeth the relevant note.

Elizabeth read through it and burst out laughing. "Oh, my dear!"

"You are happy now?" *Zarala* winked.

"Very happy." Elizabeth nodded, then grew thoughtful. "So, the fate of humans is written in this book?"

"There are many of them. Different angels guard them against the dark force. Papa let me guard this one, along with a few other books, because he knows I am interested in people who were related to me when I was a human." Her eyes twinkled. "And I am the one answering your questions when you use the *petna.*"

"Oh! But you have been very tight-lipped. And you can only guard them? You cannot change the fate of people?"

Zarala shook her head. "Papa and a council of deities assemble every day to discuss and write down people's fates, well before they are born. Once it is written, it can seldom be changed."

"That is a lot of work and responsibility. But if you do not mind me saying, your father looks very young to be the God of Gods. Indeed, he looks no more than Mr. Darcy's age."

"Oh, but Papa is thousands of years old," *Zarala* said. "Our physical appearance does not change after we grow to look like a mature adult. That is what Michael has been using to refuse me."

Elizabeth looked at her pout, and comprehension dawned. "You are in love with Michael?"

"Yes, and he has been using this age difference and the business of work issues as reasons why we cannot marry. But I seduced him, a few days ago," she confided with a proud smile. "And I have been keeping him busy. I am afraid that's why he did not respond to your calls earlier."

"Oh dear. I hope you get your heart's desire soon."

"I think he wants to earn a promotion first, before he raises the issue of marriage with Papa. He has this ridiculous notion about class differences, me being the daughter of *Zenobie* and he a hard-working angel risen from the ranks," *Zarala* said. "But enough about him, at least for now. Can you tell me more about my parents and sisters on Earth? Although I can read about them, it is nothing like hearing it from someone who knows them so well."

Elizabeth then told her about the family, both the happy events and the silly situations.

"So, may I look at the book about their fates too?" Elizabeth asked. She was extremely curious about the future.

"Oh, no, Lizzy," *Zarala* said. "Do not attempt to trick me with your innocent countenance. I could show you that little bit of Mr. Darcy's fate only because you are his guardian angel."

"Fair enough. But how did you end up here, while I ended up down on Earth? Can you tell me that at least?"

"*Zenobie*'s wife *Zelina* was taunted by *Baphoma*. Do you know of him?"

"Yes. Mr. Collins – I mean, the demon *Corcifa*– said that he is your father's twin, and that he rules the world of darkness."

"Yes. And he taunted her about being the mother of all humans while she was never truly a mother herself," *Zarala* said. "She got a bit angry and decided to take a baby from Earth to look after."

"My goodness! So she snatched you from Mrs. Bennet?"

"Yes. She told Father that she looked around for a bit, and found that I smiled and laughed a lot. She did not want a sad baby."

"But where is *Zelina* now? You refer to her as your father's wife, but not as your mother."

"When Father learned that she had interfered with the fate of humans, he was furious, and they had a big argument. That is when the crack opened and you fell to the ground. Personally, I think that Father wanted to compensate Mrs. Bennet for her loss, and did it on purpose. But she left, as well – I mean, *Zelina* did."

"She left?" Elizabeth asked. "As in … she left *Himins* for …*Baphoma*?"

"No, she left for Earth," *Zarala* said. "That is why Father can be such a softy about angels or humans in love. He still hopes to find her, one day, but she seems determined not to be found."

"Oh my. And here I thought that, as the God of all Gods, he would have no worries at all."

"Unfortunately, *Himins* is not very different from Earth, and deities have many of the same heartaches and headaches as humans."

"So he raised you himself. Did you ever want to return to Earth? You did not …resent me for taking your place?"

Zarala shook her head. "No, indeed not. I love Papa. I did not know I was once a human until Papa told me, a few years ago. I like it here, and I have been in love with Michael since I was very young. Your Mr. Darcy may be dashing, but he is too serious and quiet for my taste." She smiled and added, "You are welcome to keep him."

Elizabeth smiled and said, "To keep him in line, you mean? I shall certainly do so."

And with those last words, the two parted company.

***

Early the next morning, Mr. Darcy woke to the sight of the worried face of his sister.

"Georgiana," he said, looking around groggily.

"Fitzwilliam, are you feeling better?" Georgiana put her hand on his forehead. "The fever seems to have broken."

"And Elizabeth…?" Darcy asked.

Georgiana shook her head. "Richard is preparing to leave now for the search."

Mr. Darcy pushed the bed sheet away and tried to rise from the mattress, but the pain stopped him.

"What are you doing?" his sister demanded, steadying him. "You are far too ill to leave your bed."

"I must find Elizabeth. I shall join Richard. Wharton!" He commanded, and his valet appeared in the room immediately.

Mr. Darcy recoiled in alarm. "You are injured, Wharton," he said, seeing his valet's bandaged arm. "Go back and rest. I shall dress myself."

"Brother!" Georgiana tried to stop him, but the master and servant both seemed determined. Mr. Darcy gritted his teeth and gave his sister a silent dismissal.

"I shall change and go with you," she conceded, and left the room.

After endless minutes of struggle, Mr. Darcy was finally dressed. By the time he had completed his painful walk down the stairs, he was happy to sit down on a chair in the corridor.

Colonel Fitzwilliam came out from the morning room and looked at his cousin. He knew it was fruitless to attempt to dissuade him from participating in the search, and so he gave instructions for several men to carry Darcy out to the carriage. Georgiana followed.

It was agreed that Richard would go to Rushcliffe to locate Anne, while Georgiana would supervise the search, with the strict instruction that Mr. Darcy was only to observe from the sidelines.

The several-minute journey from the border of Pemberley to the scene of the carriage accident was a torture for Mr. Darcy. His whole body hurt like hell, and he was in despair. The chance of finding Elizabeth safe and sound was minimal. Still, he would rather stay and look at the valley that had swallowed up his beloved than stay in his bedchamber, alone.

After consulting with her brother, Georgiana instructed the servants to go down the valley in pairs in several directions. Mr. Darcy settled himself to wait on a chair by the road, reminiscing in melancholy about his acquaintance, history and love with Elizabeth. Meanwhile, Georgiana paced along the edge of the road.

An hour into the search, when no news had come, Georgiana could not hold back the tears in her eyes. She could not bear to see the grim and desperate look on her brother's face, and so she turned to lean her head on the side of the carriage, gazing back towards Pemberley on the far horizon. Even that lovely sight saddened her, for she knew that neither her home nor her brother would ever be the same without Elizabeth.

She blinked her tears away and saw, suddenly, a tiny dot of grey emerge from the valley below, some fifty yards to the left of the carriage.

Georgiana blinked several times and attempted to rub her tears away. She could now see the figure of a woman, accompanied by two servants, approaching the spot where Georgiana stood.

"Elizabeth!" The name burst from her as soon as she was certain of the woman's identity. She pelted towards her sister, while Mr. Darcy turned and tried to rise from the chair. One of the servants left Elizabeth as soon as Georgiana reached them, and ran forward to assist the Master.

"Elizabeth! You are safe!" Georgiana sobbed as she embraced her tightly. "I had nearly lost all hope."

"Yes, Georgiana, I myself feared for the worst, for a while," Elizabeth said.

"Are you hurt?" Georgiana asked, finally calming herself enough to take a good look at her.

"Just scratches and bruises, and a bump on the head. I think I must have wandered off in another direction, dazed, when I regained consciousness from the fall. I did not see your brother or the servants. I tried to climb up but could not find the way, so I took shelter under a big tree for the night. Luckily, the weather was not too cold."

"Eliza...beth!" Leaning heavily on the arm of the servant, Mr. Darcy finally reached them.

"Fitzwilliam!"

They stared at each other for more than a minute, their hearts in their eyes, before they embraced each other tightly.

Mr. Darcy drew in a deep breath, ignoring the pain in his body, but an overwhelmingly invigorating feeling filled his heart. Then the worry, the fear, and the trauma of the past day finally took their toll on him, and he fainted.

Elizabeth and Georgiana gasped in alarm, and the servants rushed to support the Master. They carried him to the carriage. Then, as soon as the women had joined him, the carriage pulled out, making its way back to Pemberley with slow care.

Georgiana was sobbing again. Elizabeth, too, had tears running down her face but she was calm. She knew that her beloved would be fine. His head rested on her lap in the carriage, and she smoothed his wayward hair and blotted the sweat from his forehead. Looking at his tired, battered face, emotion welled up within her afresh.

In truth, he might have been prideful when she first met him. But he had proved himself to be a good man, one who loved her fervently and wanted to protect her against Mr. Wickham, the kidnappers and the demon. He had taken good care of his sister, his servants and his tenants. She was honoured to be his wife, and she would willingly forfeit her angelic status and spend a lifetime with him, bearing his children and growing old with him.

She kissed his closed eyelids and prayed for him to wake up soon.

Not long thereafter, they reached the house. The Master was carried carefully to his bedchamber, and was soon attended to by the doctor. Mrs. Reynolds burst into tears when she saw that the Mistress was safe. She insisted that Mrs. Darcy take a quick bath and have her scratches and bruises treated, before allowing her to go to her husband.

He woke up not long after the doctor's ministration, but when he did not immediately see his wife again, he panicked. Despite the doctor's and Wharton's protests, he raised himself and had the two reluctant men assist him as he went to knock on the door to the Mistress's chamber.

A refreshed Elizabeth greeted him, and he embraced her tightly, savoring the presence of his beloved in his arms.

"Fitzwilliam, let us get you back to the bed. You must get some rest or you may faint again," she said.

"Do not leave me," he entreated.

"I shall stay with you," she promised, and had the two men assist him back to the Master's chamber. Once he was settled, and the doctor had reassured her that her husband would soon be fit again if he rested for a few days, she dismissed everyone and stretched out by his side.

He hugged her tightly, inhaling the sweet lavender scent of her body. Then he traced his fingertips along her cheek and jaw, as if to engrave the angles of her face into his mind. With an unsteady voice, he recounted the horrors of the day before. "I had feared that it was time for you to return to Heaven, when Richard said they could not find you after the accident."

She kissed his fingers tenderly, deciding to be open with him. "Indeed, I did go to *Himins*."

"What?" His eyes widened and he smoothed his hands down her shoulders to make sure she was real. "But you are here. Does that mean that *Zenobie* will allow you to stay on Earth? Forever?"

"How did you know that there was such a possibility?"

"I learned of it from Michael, the night before your fight with Mr. Collins."

She smiled down at him. "Yes. I argued my case, and I am allowed to stay here with you."

Mr. Darcy had not expected such wonderful news, after a day of such horrible events. He burst out crying, like a young boy, sobbing in Elizabeth's embrace, at last daring to believe that their life was going to be bliss.

When he finally calmed, he asked her to tell him about her trip to Heaven. "So, the earthly Elizabeth Bennet is sound and well in *Himins*, and has fallen in love with Michael?" he asked when her tale was at an end.

"Yes. She is a charming and decisive woman."

"Very much like you," he said, and then a look of tremulous hope dawned in his eyes. "And we may have children, one day?"

She smiled brightly and caressed his chest. "That is a possibility. You have to get well soon, so that we can work on that together."

He drew in a deep breath, feeling the blood stir in his body, but he was too tired and weak to participate yet. Instead, he pinched her bottom lightly. "Teasing woman!"

She winked at him, then turned serious. "What are we to do about Anne and Lydia?"

"We must hope that Richard finds her before Wickham marries her," he spat. "I do not want him to control Anne's life and wealth for his own wicked pleasure."

"I hope so, too. And Lydia? We cannot go to London yet, not for a few days, at least, until you are strong enough. Will Mrs. Younge harm her?"

"Wharton is injured and deserves some rest. Let me ask Mrs. Reynolds to bring a few men to locate the shameless woman and keep an eye on your sister when she finds Mrs. Younge. We will inform your father of the news, as well." He summoned the housekeeper and did that immediately afterwards.

"I hope Father will not do anything hasty," Elizabeth said as she sealed the letter for Mrs. Reynolds to take to her uncle's house in Gracechurch Street.

After the instructions were given, the couple rested, at Georgiana's and Mrs. Reynolds's insistence. The newlyweds awoke late in the evening to the news that Colonel Fitzwilliam had returned – and he had found his cousin.

"How is Anne?" Mr. Darcy asked. They were holding the meeting in the Master chamber, as Darcy was still too weak to dress. Elizabeth sat on a chair at his bedside.

"She was exhausted and sad," the Colonel replied grimly. "She did not want to come with me at first, so...well, I lied, and told her that Wickham had been seen leaving Rustcliffe for London because he was going to marry Miss Lydia."

"Did she believe you?" Elizabeth asked.

Richard shook his head. "At first she did not. She thought he loved her and that, because she was so much richer, there was no reason for Wickham to choose Miss Lydia over her. We waited for over three hours at the Inn but, when the scoundrel did not show his face, her belief in him started to crumble. I confess that I was very harsh and told her that Wickham must have preferred a more robust woman for his life's companion. Maybe he would return to marry her once he had settled Miss Lydia in London well enough. That was when Anne finally relented and agreed to come with me back to Pemberley for the night, instead of staying in the Inn."

"Oh no. Anne must be heartbroken," Georgiana exclaimed. "But why did you mention the blackguard wanting to marry Elizabeth's sister?"

Mr. Darcy looked at his wife and, when she nodded, he said, "I told Richard, this morning, before he left for Rushcliffe, about Miss Lydia's situation. She is said to have eloped with Wickham, and was traced as far as London – but not beyond."

"Scoundrel!" Georgiana's face turned bright red. "He is intent on hurting every innocent woman who crosses his path."

"I shall be the first to strangle him when he crosses *my* path," Colonel Fitzwilliam said, and gulped down the glass of wine.

"What are we to do with Anne?"

"I propose to take her to Matlock. Father and Mother should be back from London soon. At least Mother will know what to do concerning her condition," Colonel Fitzwilliam said.

"Georgiana, will you go with Anne or do you want to come with us to London?" Darcy asked. "Elizabeth and I shall travel there, once I feel better, to help find Miss Lydia."

"I shall go with Anne," Georgiana decided. "And I shall do my best to cheer her up."

"You believe that Miss Lydia is in London?" Colonel Fitzwilliam asked. "Wickham has not been seen in Rushcliffe for several days now. Perhaps he has another meeting planned in a different place in Derbyshire with Miss Lydia."

"It would not be so easy for Lydia to travel two days alone to Derbyshire without being noticed," Elizabeth said, cautious not to reveal the information she had learned in *Himins* to the two other people in the room. "But, judging from the letter I received from Jane, Lydia was last sighted in London, not on coaches leaving for anywhere."

The next morning, Colonel Fitzwilliam left with Anne and Georgiana. Mrs. Jenkinson was dismissed without reference. The Darcys rested for another two days before undertaking the journey to London, having received no news from Mrs. Reynolds or Mr. Bennet in the meantime.

CHAPTER SEVENTEEN

Wickham sat in the tavern near Edward Street in London, cursing *Zenobie*, Michael and *Himins*.

Bloody Zenobie, withholding the truth, did not warn me of the full consequences of my choice. And that stupid Michael is in cahoots with him. I thought he was my friend.

He swallowed another mouthful of the cheap wine.

Since his descent to Earth, he had met with one dire happenstance after another. First, the great man from *Himins* had set him down in the middle of a pig farm, nowhere near Rustcliffe. He had had to endure all the rotten smells and the undesirable smears of waste all over his body, incurred while he was trying to escape a beating from a farm girl.

He was sure, if he had just been his usual charming self, that he could easily have persuaded that pretty peasant to submit to his seduction. Instead, she had chased him away from her farm with a pitchfork.

He then had to walk over three miles along muddy lanes until he finally found his way back to the nearest village. Passing farm carts and carriages showed him no mercy; for once, no one seemed willing to give him a lift.

The nearest village was nearly ten miles south of Rustcliffe. Luckily, he still had some money in his pocket, more than enough to secure a room in which to clean himself up. But the coach did not arrive at Rustcliffe until very late, and he could not find his prize bride-to-be, Miss de Bourgh.

After some enquiries, he learned that Anne had left with a colonel for Pemberley. He paid someone to pass a message to her but, after waiting in Rustcliffe for two days without news, he decided that he had better secure the next best thing, Miss Lydia.

He was willing to bet that Darcy would settle him well in exchange for agreeing to disappear from Miss Lydia's life, so he journeyed to London in haste. But when he had arrived at Edward Street, last evening, Mrs. Younge told him that she had put Lydia in another guest house, one belonging to her friend, because the girl was too troublesome, demanding to know his whereabouts all the time. Coyly, she informed him that she would not reveal Lydia's new location unless he paid her in kind.

Mr. Wickham was annoyed by the delay but happy to oblige. After all, they had been together, on and off, for some years. Mrs. Younge was not bad looking, except that she never allowed him to climax inside her, for fear of pregnancy.

But he was outraged and mortified by the next turn of events: he could not get a rise, even after trying for almost an hour. *Zenobie* must have had something to do with it. Even his tongue could not give his partner her usual satisfaction. She wanted him hard and inside of her, but little Wickham was limp and uncooperative, no matter how he tried.

At that, she became angry with him and tied him to the bed while he was distracted. With the help of a riding crop, she whipped him until she finally drew some response from his little man.

Mr. Wickham suffered through the encounter in silence, enduring the physical pain of the whip against his soft flesh, and the verbal lash of her abuse over his inadequacy. She only released him late in the evening, and demanded that he pay her in coin, as well, for the trouble she had taken while hosting Lydia – either that or agree to come back to satisfy her again for a week. She would only reveal Lydia's whereabouts then.

He gritted his teeth as he left Younge's lodging. The amount of money she demanded was ridiculous, and his plan to secure *Lizzybell*'s sister was delayed yet again. He was sure it was *Zenobie*'s doing. How could he, Wickham – the seducer, the charmer, the great lover of Pemberley and of Cambridge – be having manly problems? He had never had a problem of that sort before, in all of his many years of trifling with women. *Zenobie* had cheated him!

On that unhappy thought, Wickham went to a nearby tavern, intending to drown his sorrows. A few men invited him to join them at cards, and he lost heavily. *What will my life be if I cannot win at cards and cannot bed women as I like?*

He gulped down another mouthful and decided to try his charms on the maid. She had curly brown hair and a lively expression, reminding him of *Lizzybell*.

"Hello there, gorgeous girl. When are you finishing here?" He smiled, pretending to gaze at her with devotion.

The girl looked him up and down and replied, in a surprisingly educated voice, "None of your business."

With that, she raised her head and walked past him.

What?! Even a lowly tavern maid has given me the snub. Wickham was angry, and so he followed her quietly out to the back of the tavern, where he pinched her buttocks playfully and pressed her against the wall. "Come along, my pretty wench, let me satisfy you."

The woman screamed at the top of her voice and hit him hard on the chest, in one of the many spots where he was still hurting from Mrs. Young's beating. He let go of her immediately.

"What're yo doin' to our Sarah?" Two men emerged from the tavern, carrying bottles and raising their voices at him.

"Damn!" Wickham swore, and fled the place immediately. With his luck of late, there was no telling whether he might have been killed by those seedy men.

He walked for hours, cursing, until he had utterly lost track of his way. The townhouses around him were big and elegant, by now. The sight of them made him feel sorry for himself again. He could have had all the wealth and women in the world, if only he had not squandered the money that Darcy had given him from his father's will, or if he had managed to marry Georgiana or Anne. So many lost opportunities, and he was now standing on the other side of all of that wealth. Even his charm with women and his luck at the gaming tables were gone. Life was too cruel!

Suddenly, the back door of a townhouse opened, and an elegantly dressed woman slipped out and walked on, with unsteady steps.

Where is she going? A rich lady walking in London in the middle of the night? Meeting a lover?

A scheme came into his mind. He would play rough, kidnap the lady, have his wicked way with her, and then demand hush money from her family.

As they came to a deserted lane, he wrapped one arm around the woman's waist from behind and clamped his hand over her mouth.

"Ah!" Wickham screamed in pain and let go of the woman as he felt her biting his hand. When she turned round to confront him, he realised that he recognised her from his acquaintance with her brother during Cambridge days. "Miss Bingley?"

"I am Mrs. Darcy. Who are you? What do you want?"

"Mrs. Darcy?" Wickham looked at her dazed countenance. "Mrs. Darcy is the former Elizabeth Bennet. Are you out of your ...?"

He had not even finished the sentence when the woman flung herself at him, pushing him against the wall with surprising strength. "You know that country upstart. You conspired with her to take Mr. Darcy away from me."

Wickham's head cracked hard against the wall, and he lost consciousness as Miss Bingley used her reticule to strike him repeatedly.

When Mr. Hurst found his lost sister some time later, attacking a man on a deserted lane, he had no choice but to send her to Scarborough and set her up in a separate establishment immediately. He hired two nurses to keep a close watch on her at all times.

As for the young man, he regained consciousness at the doctor's establishment but could not tell anyone who he was. He kept insisting that he was an angel whose duty it was to make women pregnant and cheat at cards. He also cursed some people named *Zenobie* and Michael, and insisted stridently that Miss Bingley was not Mrs. Darcy. As the man seemed to know his sister, Mr. Hurst made arrangements to keep him locked away in a private room in Bedlam. At least, in that way, Mr. Hurst could be assured that Miss Bingley's victim would not harm the Bingley family's reputation.

***

Three Years Later...

Mr. Darcy turned his head to one side and frowned. Then he threw down his pen in haste, hurried out of the study, and dashed to the library. The footmen and servants had become used to the sight of such actions by the Master since he married.

Once inside the library, he locked the door and called out, "Yes, my dear angel? What can I do for you now?"

"Come to me, Fitzwilliam. I am here." The sound of his wife was heard behind the last shelves.

The corners of his mouth turned up as he walked to her slowly, surveying the shelves as he moved through the huge library.

When he reached the end of the room without spotting her, he was ready to call out again. But then he remembered her antics and lifted his gaze. There she was, with her wings spread, floating at the level of the tallest shelves, book in hand, her face flushed, laughing at him with her eyes.

His breath quickened as he bowed formally to her and repeated, "Yes, my dear angel? What can I do for you now?"

"Your grandfather collected some deeply interesting books. This one makes me want to…"

"Want to do what?" Darcy asked, pretending not to understand her intent.

Elizabeth bit her lip and said, "You already know what I want. You locked the door."

He folded his arms. "I know I am to do your bidding now, whenever you want, as a punishment for my wicked demands before our marriage. But I prefer to have clear instructions, to prevent any misunderstanding."

"Insufferable man!" She flew to another shelf, where the tall ladder was. "Climb the ladder and join me up here."

A grin adorned his face as he shrugged out of his coat, pulled his neck cloth out, and unbuttoned his waistcoat and shirt.

Her eyes widened and she asked in a husky voice, "What are you doing?"

"Your bidding, my love. It is dangerous to undress high up on the ladder." He replied in a matter-of-fact tone, but his heart was pounding. When he pulled off his boots and stripped off his breeches, he could see that his wife was devouring his naked form with hungry eyes. His arousal stirred to life immediately.

As he climbed up the ladder, his gaze never left his wife. By the time he reached the top and sat down, eye to eye with her, she was breathing hard and her wings flapping fast.

"Kiss me," she whispered, and leaned towards him.

He did not need more instruction from his Mistress. He wrapped a hand around her waist and touched her soft lips, slowly at first. Savouring her sweet taste, he started suckling them, then thrust his tongue into her mouth.

Her hands flew around his back, and the book in question dropped to the floor with a thump as she used both hands to knead the muscles of his back.

He pulled the sleeves off her shoulders and bared her ample bosom. His mouth abandoned hers and moved to taste her twin peaks. As he shaped and squeezed her creamy mounds and plucked the nipples hard, her loud moans were music to his ears.

His hands wandered down to cup her pert buttocks, and he slid a finger from the base of her spine down the crease of her buttocks, moving over the sleek fabric of her dress.

She shivered under his ministration and flew even closer to him, settling her legs around his waist. "Make love to me," she panted.

He drew in a deep breath, pushed his hands under her dress and traced his fingers along the inside of her thighs, brushed against her apex and stirring her secret folds. She gasped and pressed her body yet closer, wet and ready.

"Always," he replied.

He lowered her onto his hard shaft, pushing his way in slowly, inch by inch. They held their breath, and the library became eerily silent during this slow journey, until he reached her hilt and they became one flesh.

Mr. Darcy looked at his wife. Her hair was disheveled, and a few wayward strands were plastered against her damp forehead. He loved the feeling of being fully sheathed inside her, her soft muscles squeezing his hard ones.

Kissing her tenderly on the mouth, he wiped the dew of perspiration from her forehead and began to grind into her, pulling out only slightly, then thrusting and rubbing in circular motions.